ONE SMALL STEP FOR MAN . . . ONE QUANTUM LEAP FOR MANKIND

Theorizing that a man could time travel within his own lifetime, Dr. Sam Beckett stepped into the Quantum Leap Accelerator—and vanished.

Somehow he was transported not only in time, but into *someone else's* life. . . .

And the Quantum Leap Project took on a whole new dimension.

QUANTUM LEAP

Now all the excitement and originality of the acclaimed television show are captured in these independent novels . . . all-new adventures, all-new leaps!

**OUT OF TIME. OUT OF BODY.
OUT OF CONTROL.**

QUANTUM LEAP

TOO CLOSE FOR COMFORT

A NOVEL BY
ASHLEY McCONNELL
BASED ON THE UNIVERSAL TELEVISION
SERIES "QUANTUM LEAP"
CREATED BY DONALD P. BELLISARIO

ACE BOOKS, NEW YORK

Quantum Leap: Too Close for Comfort, a novel by Ashley McConnell, based on the Universal television series QUANTUM LEAP, created by Donald P. Bellisario.

This book is an Ace original edition, and has never been previously published.

QUANTUM LEAP: TOO CLOSE FOR COMFORT

An Ace Book / published by arrangement with MCA Publishing Rights, a Division of MCA, Inc.

PRINTING HISTORY
Ace edition / April 1993

ISBN: 0–441–69323–7

Ace Books are published by The Berkley Publishing Group,
200 Madison Avenue, New York, New York 10016.
The name "ACE" and the "A" logo are trademarks
belonging to Charter Communications, Inc.

PRINTED IN THE UNITED STATES OF AMERICA

10 9 8 7 6 5 4 3 2 1

ACKNOWLEDGMENTS

The author gratefully acknowledges the support and assistance of Kathryn Ptacek and all those others without whom writing would not be a Possible Thing. Particularly, in this case, Presbyterian Urgent Care Center.

AUTHOR'S NOTE

The timing of this Leap is, of course, prior to the one recorded in the television episode "A Leap for Lisa."

June 22, 1990

CHAPTER
ONE

Thump thump thump. *Thump* thump thump.

"Hey *yaaaa!*"

For a moment, he thought he might have Leaped right out of his own theory, into some Plains Indian dance of the last century. Or, he reminded himself as someone jogged into him, sending him staggering, maybe a Plains Indian dance of the current century. He'd been to a powwow once. At least, he thought he had. . . .

The muttering of the line of men stacking up behind him brought the situation back into focus, and he shuffled forward, sneaking glances around himself.

No, this couldn't be a powwow. He was in a line of perhaps thirty bare-chested men dancing, two steps forward, one step back, in an irregular circle, in a poorly lighted room that probably housed conferences in another life. There were a couple of

Hispanics, but the majority were definitely Anglos. *Not* a powwow.

The men shook six-foot-long dowel sticks above their heads as they grunted and yelled, sticks painted and bound with brightly colored fluffy feathers that no real bird could have flown with. They were stripped to the waist, revealing chests hairy and smooth, fish-belly pale and bronzed, jellied and solid. They were otherwise dressed in shorts and slacks, normal street wear, but their feet were bare. They all looked to be in their late thirties to early sixties. And they'd been dancing long enough to have worked up a sweat; the room reeked.

He looked around in vain for a mirror, grunting out of sync with the rest. There wasn't one available; the room was almost featureless except for the chandelier glittering on half power over their heads. It looked a lot like a hotel banquet room before anybody came in to set it up.

Holding his breath, he looked down at himself and gave an unobtrusive sigh of relief. Definitely male this time, in pretty good shape. At least he didn't have to worry about *that* complication. This body seemed to be younger than most of the others he could see out of the corner of his eye; it felt healthy, if a bit on the scrawny side. He could see his ribs if he looked hard enough. He was wearing jeans, but like the others in the group his upper body and feet were bare.

The man behind him slapped him on the shoulder, urging him forward, and he ducked his head in apology and grunted onward.

At one end of the room, on a low platform, a man wearing rough leather trousers and a fringed vest beat on a tall drum with a heavy-knobbed stick. The walls of the room were insulated with cork. *And a good thing too,* he thought, yelling "Hey *yaaa!*"

One beat too late. He winced. A few of the others glared at him, but the circle was breaking up and the men were crowding toward the platform, jostling him along. He found himself in the front, staring up at the drummer.

The drummer was in his early sixties, the hair on his barrel chest skimpy and gleaming silver, his beard growing out past neatness, his hairline receded from the pink pate. He set the instrument aside carefully, as if it were a fragile thing, and laid the drumstick across the drum head lightly, as if it would be dangerous if it somehow made a sound when it wasn't supposed to. He wore glasses with dark, heavy rims, and his eyes were almost hidden in the distortion of the thick lenses.

"My brothers," he said. Surprisingly, his voice was a light tenor. "You are all my brothers."

Oh no, he thought. *Not that. Please, anything but—*

"We are gathered here to remember what it is to be Men!" The speaker would have roared, but a fit of coughing caught him as he raised a fist in the air. Before him, the audience politely ignored the speaker's rapidly purpling face and growled in response, "We are Men!"

Sam Beckett, who was sometimes a man and sometimes not, lunged onto the platform and slapped the speaker hard on the back to clear his windpipe. The older man gasped and nodded, clinging to the rim of the drum for balance.

"Are you okay?" Sam asked, as the other man slowly straightened up again and set his glasses back on his nose. The audience was watching the two of them with bland interest, waiting for the next cue.

"Get back down there, Ross," the speaker whispered. Sam hesitated an instant, then obeyed, watching out of the corner of his eye to make sure, first, that he wouldn't have to apply the Heimlich maneuver, and second, that he was supposed to respond to that name. The older man nodded sagely, reassuring him.

Ross, he thought. *This time my name is Ross.*

The press of men retreated a little to let him step back among them, and he tried to fade into the circle, become a part of it. There were too many still looking at him, however, to let him be unobtrusive. He hoped that he wasn't expected to lead any chants or calisthenics.

It was one of those men's encounter groups. That would make it—he rummaged frantically in his faulty memory—late eighties. Very late eighties, or early nineties. He vaguely remembered a book coming out in late 1990 about some kind of fairy tale for men, but men were having spiritual retreats to find their "inner child" even before then.

The speaker was still making pronouncements, thrusting his fist in the air, and the men around him were responding in a liturgy of grunting affirmations.

Somewhere in the New Mexico desert, on this very day, he realized, Sam Beckett was burrowing into a cave, building a computer to end all computers, outlining a theory of time travel and strings, shoes

6

and ships and sealing wax and cabbages and kings. The Sam Beckett in the desert had no clue that somewhere else, in a hotel meeting room, among two or three dozen half-naked, sweating, smelly men, another Sam Beckett occupied the body of someone named Ross.

He could leave this room, find a telephone, call himself up, and tell himself not to build the neurocells that made up the "hybrid computer," not to build the Accelerator, not to step into it, not to begin the process of Leaping.

He wondered what would happen if he did that.

Maybe he'd already started Leaping. Could he Leap in two places at once?

The men were spreading out again, making a new circle, sitting on the floor and facing inward.

If he could be in two places at once, in the desert and here, why not three? Four? A dozen?

He shook his head. He didn't know, but there wasn't enough of him to go around as it was.

The circle of men placed the flat of their hands on the floor in front of them, leaned into them, swayed back. The swaying was ragged, some of the men more a part of the activity than others. It made him feel a little better. There were several who were sliding sideways looks to their neighbors, just as he was, in an effort to do the right thing at the right time. One man, especially, at the far edge of his vision, was always a little behind. It was hard to see; the chandelier was operated on a dimmer switch, and the shifting crowd cast odd shadows against the wall.

There must be some good reason why he couldn't be in three places at the same time. Something about

7

his body being in one, and his mind in another, and nothing left over to be in a third. It was reassuring somehow to know that there *were* limits.

Maybe it also meant there would be a natural end to his Leaping, someday, when he ran out of times to Leap into.

"And they say you only live once," he muttered.

"Men," the ex-drummer said sententiously, "are more than they think they are."

Sam rolled his eyes.

"Men are strong!"

There was something he was supposed to change. There was always something he was supposed to change: he hoped he wasn't supposed to put some poor guy in touch with his masculinity. He wondered where Al was. Now there was a guy who never had any problems about his masculinity.

If he could get out of here and find a shirt, he could call the Project and talk to himself.

Except he couldn't remember his telephone number at the Project. Area code 505 . . . something. It had to be 505. The whole state of New Mexico was 505. He was almost sure.

It was maddening, having a photographic memory with holes in the negative.

The men in the circle folded their arms across their chests, closed their eyes, and bowed their heads. They swayed back and forth, and a low, deep humming vibrated through the line.

"Remember what it was like to be a boy?" the tenor voice said. "Remember the first time you saw your father."

It was a command, and Sam remembered his father: huge, bulky, breath wheezing, skin already

8

mottled by too much time in the sun, hands with large blunt fingers sliding across the flank of a cow, fitting copper tubing in place, twisting a key in the ignition of the old pickup. He smelled of tobacco and sweat and the cheese sandwiches he'd had for lunch.

"How old were you when you saw your father for the first time, and knew him?"

He could feel those hands across his back, holding him up over his head. He could hear sounds. Not words yet. This person, this man, was someone special to him. He knew that. He was . . . four months old. *Dad,* he thought, and a spasm of sorrow clenched in his chest.

"To know yourself as Men, you must know your fathers. You must know your sons. Let that be the lesson of this circle. Remember, and teach."

"What if you haven't got any kids?" the man next to Sam asked, sotto voce.

The leader heard him. "If you have no sons, remember for the sons you will one day have." A thud from the drum punctuated the reprimand. "Let the circle break."

As the lights came up, Sam heard the swoosh of the Door opening, and looked around for Al. The mass of middle-aged men disintegrated as individuals staggered to their feet and drifted over to the duffel bags stacked against the walls, digging out towels and shoes and socks and shirts, getting dressed again. They weren't talking to each other much. There was some self-conscious laughter when one man tripped over his dowel stick.

He couldn't find Al.

Al should have shown up by this time.

He was looking around when the leader stepped down from the platform and took him by the arm.

"Ross," he said, "thank you. You were a great help to me."

"Oh, sure." He didn't want to brush off the other man, but he wanted to find Al to find out what he was supposed to be doing.

Al was from his own time—a dozen years, plus or minus a couple—in the future. Al, linked to him through that hybrid computer he was building even as he stood in the here-and-now in the body of a young man named Ross, was supposed to tell him who and where he was and what he had to do to get out of here.

"I'll be talking to some of the newer members of our circle now. It will be a little while before we go home." The leader smiled, patted his arm, and moved away.

Before we go home? Sam thought. *Huh? What have I gotten myself into this time? Is this my father, or—*

"There you are," came Al's voice from behind him.

"Oh good," Sam said, turning. "Hey, what's with the plainclothes? Are you in disguise, or—"

Al was looking at him, puzzled, as he pulled on a white shirt and buttoned the cuffs. "Are you talking to me, kid?"

"Of course I am—" He stopped, staring. This was Al, his friend, his Observer, his partner on the Project. Al had never shown up half-dressed before. Why was Al putting on a shirt?

"Oh, holy hell." The same familiar, gravelly voice came from the other side, in stereo.

Sam spun around. "Al?"

On the one hand, the Al now tucking the shirttail into his waistband said impatiently, "What?"

On the other, another Al, this one dressed in a dapper dark green suit with a lighter green shirt, a festive red tie, and a fedora with a sprig of mistletoe pinned to the band, stared over Sam's shoulder, his face far too pale for the colors he was wearing. "That's . . . that's me."

The Observer's hand was shaking ever so slightly. The lights on the handlink he held in his right hand shimmered on his face.

"Al?" Sam whispered.

"Yeah, kid, what's the problem? Look, if this Dr. Wales wants to talk to me he's going to have to get with the program."

Sam tore his attention away from the appalled Observer to the man buckling his belt in front of him. Al Calavicci, a short, slender man with a southern Italian olive complexion, dark hair, dark eyes under bushy eyebrows, stood on either side of him. The Al Calavicci who had just finished getting dressed looked tired, thin. There were dark circles under his eyes, and he was checking his watch and looking around with sharp, brittle movements. "C'mon, I've got things to do." He glared at Sam—or rather, the body that Sam had Leaped into. "You got a problem, kid? What're you staring at?"

"I never expected to see you here," Sam said honestly.

Al's eyebrows knit. He opened his mouth, then reconsidered whatever he had planned to say. "Neither did I," he muttered, more to himself than to Sam. "Damn silly if you ask me. Wales!" His voice rose as he looked around for the group leader.

Sam turned back to the Observer. "Al?" He remembered just in time to lower his voice, and tried to herd the man with the handlink over to the wall, out of the stream of circle participants heading out the door.

Herding didn't work, of course. Instead of guiding him out of the crowd, he walked right through the oblivious Observer. Al-the-Observer was present only in a hologrammatic image. His physical body stood in the Imaging Chamber of the Project, years in the future. The image that appeared in the past was tuned to Sam Beckett. No one else in the room could see or hear him. Including, apparently, himself.

Al-the-Observer was more shaken than Sam had ever seen him. The man in green was still staring after the man in the knit shirt and new, crisp-looking khaki slacks. "This isn't possible," he said.

He tried to lift the cigar in his right hand to his mouth, lifted his left hand holding the handlink instead, fumbled.

The handlink slipped out of his hand. As it lost contact with his flesh, the Observer disappeared.

CHAPTER
TWO

The lights were up full by now, and Sam stood by the wall alone, abruptly aware that he wasn't doing anything, including getting dressed, and his lack of activity was making him conspicuous. Al was heading for the small cluster of men around Dr. Wales, leaving "Ross" staring alternately after him and at a hole in the air. With some effort Sam closed his slackened jaw and followed the Al that remained.

"I think we made real progress here this afternoon," Dr. Wales was saying, peering around at his disciples. A faint accent flavored his words, and Sam strained unsuccessfully to identify it. Wales hadn't put a shirt on yet either, and his chest was stark white. His arms, by contrast, were the dark tan of a man who often wore short-sleeved shirts outdoors. It made him look as if he were wearing a shirt of his own skin. "Just imagine, three months ago there were only a few of us. . . ." He looked up and caught sight of Sam.

"Ross!" Smiling, he took Sam's arm and pulled him into the circle of men. "This boy—this *man*, I should say"—the remark was greeted with friendly chuckles—"he's been an incredible help to me. I couldn't do this without him. He drives me around, runs errands for me. He's a good boy, this Ross Malachy."

"I thought you said he was a man," came a familiar growl from the perimeter of the circle.

Wales nodded. "Yes. Yes, Al, he is. But when I look at Ross, I see myself as I once was, as I want to be still, and that image for me is the boy, still learning, still searching for wisdom. I call him a boy. For me he will always be a boy because he is so much younger. But in truth he is a man—learning to be a man, like all the rest of us."

"*I* already know." Sam wasn't certain Wales had heard Al's response, though it was clear that some of the others had. They edged away, leaving him isolated outside the circle. Al's sharp, dark eyes took note of the movement of the people around him, and a shadow that could have represented a shrug, or a sneer, flitted across his face. After a moment he turned away from the group, as if it held nothing more for him.

"We'll see you at our next meeting," Wales said in farewell.

Al didn't respond. But the group leader seemed certain, and turned back to the rest, unruffled by the rejection. "Once contact with your inner self, your inner child, has been established, it must be nurtured, cared for, or it will not grow, you will have no benefit from it. Some men say that this is a feminine trait, and belongs to Women—" Sam could hear the

14

capitals in his voice—"but it is also the place of Men to nurture, to support, to teach each other. This is an essential part of the process of knowing ourselves, of learning to value what it is to be a Man."

Al walked out the door.

Wales continued to talk to the other men, completely absorbed in his lecture, and eventually Sam worked his way out of the circle and the room. As he had surmised, the room was a hotel banquet room. The hallway was empty. A few feet away, across the lobby, glass doors led to a half-full parking lot outside. Reflected sunlight glittered on windshields and chrome; the sky was a pure, cloudless blue.

A small child clad in a pink playsuit, ran past on the sidewalk outside the door and skidded to a stop as she caught sight of him. With the nonchalance of a typical four-year-old, she shielded her eyes and pressed her face against the glass to get a better look. Sam grinned and waved. The little girl giggled and waved back and ran away.

The looks on the faces of the adults who followed the child a moment later reminded him that he was still half-dressed. He went back inside the banquet room to find Wales shrugging heavily into a sleeveless shirt, and the other men getting ready to leave. There was only one knapsack left, half-hidden against the edge of the platform, and Sam deduced that it must belong to Ross Malachy. He reached for it, casually, ready to turn it over to someone else if challenged, but no one said anything, and inside he found a shirt, a battered leather wallet, keys, and spare change. He checked his pockets—empty. Evidently one of the rules for the gathering was not carrying anything. Now that the meeting was over

15

he felt justified in loading his pockets again.

The driver's license picture showed a pale young man—September 12, 1970 was the date of birth—with curling black hair and eyes so blue he didn't even have to read the data entry. It was a New Mexico license; the address was in the northeast quadrant of Albuquerque.

A chill ran up his spine. *I'm probably less than three hundred miles away from myself right this minute,* he thought.

The license was issued in 1988, and was due to expire in 1992. Assuming that Ross Malachy was a law-abiding citizen who hadn't moved recently, he knew approximately where and when he was, and he even had a home address. He closed his eyes, trying to remember if there was anything exciting happening in Albuquerque during that four-year period. Albuquerque itself wasn't all that exciting to begin with—it was the largest city in New Mexico, and home to the premium weapons-engineering laboratory in the country and maybe in the world, but less than a half million people lived there. The university was probably best known for its basketball team, and even that wasn't saying much. Santa Fe, the state capital, was much more glamorous.

He couldn't remember. He couldn't tell if that was because his faulty memory was giving out on him again, or if Albuquerque was just a boring place to be; it was probably his memory. When he tried to pin it down, he caught mental glimpses of tunnels and lights and construction equipment, memories that he was pretty sure were of the building phase of the Project. And that wasn't in Albuquerque at all, though he'd had to travel through it every time he went back to Washington with Al to beg for funding to keep going.

The time defined by the driver's license fit his earlier estimate. He was awfully close to his own time. In terms of Leap years—his years, that is—he had no idea how much time had passed at the Project while he had been Leaping from one person's body to another. He knew, from comments Al had let slip, that time passed at a different rate for him than it did for the people at the Project. His own observations—when he remembered about them—indicated that the delta, the rate of change, wasn't a constant. The process of Leaping tore holes in his memory, and sometimes he could recall things that in the last Leap, or the next, would be totally blank.

"Time to go," Wales said cheerfully, coming over to slap him on the back. "I think it went very well, don't you?"

"Oh sure, sure," he said automatically. Al hadn't looked as if it were going well—neither Al-the-Observer or—what was he supposed to call him? Real-Al? It didn't work, somehow. Sam wondered if he would experience the same shock in seeing himself that Al obviously had. He'd Leaped *into* himself once, seen himself as a boy looking at himself in a mirror; but the difference in age made it easier, somehow, to feel that this "other person" really was someone else, a *different* person. The Al that Al was seeing was only a few years younger. There was less of an age difference between Al-the-Observer and Al-the-Observed than there was between Al-the-Observer and Sam himself. It was a different kind of shock.

A smug small voice in the back of his mind remarked, *Now he knows how I feel when I look in the mirror and I'm not there.*

Wales was waiting for him, impatiently. He managed to lag behind to catch a glimpse of the headlines on a newspaper in a dispenser near the lobby door. *The Albuquerque Journal* for Friday, June 22, 1990, read: "House Kills Flag-Burning Amendment. At Least 25,000 Killed as Quake Pounds Iran. Missing Los Lunas Teens OK. Gay Community Said 'Relapsing' into Unsafe Sex."

It was unlikely that he was here to change any of those things.

"Okay," he said. "At least it narrows the possibilities."

The older man, heading for a red Blazer, was looking over his shoulder for Sam, and Sam jogged to catch up, fumbling in his pocket for the car keys. The late-afternoon, late-spring/late-summer sun was blazing hot, even with a whisper of breeze in the air. He paused for a moment to look up at the sky, recalling New Mexican weather. No clouds gathering— that much was typical for June. Earlier in the year, say in March, the winds would be miserable; later, in July and August, storm clouds would be boiling out of the mountains to dump fifteen minutes' worth of torrential rains over the Rio Grande valley. But it was hotter than he would have expected; even with the low humidity, the temperature must be up in the nineties.

Starting the engine, he closed his eyes for a moment, relating the address on the driver's license to his patchy memory of the city's layout. With Wales in the passenger seat beside him, he couldn't very well pull out a map to find out where Ross Malachy lived. He was assuming Malachy lived close to

Wales, which wasn't a good assumption to make, but still. . . .

"Go to the university first, please," Wales said, interrupting Sam's train of thought. "I want to drop something off."

With a sigh of relief, Sam headed down the road. He knew where the University of New Mexico was, even though he'd never taught or taken classes there; it had a library, and that was enough to imprint it in his memory. Besides, the city was laid out on a grid, and the university was almost exactly in the middle. He turned so that the mountains were at his back and followed the main thoroughfares to Central Avenue, the old Route 66. From there it was just a matter of following the signs.

Parking was, of course, another problem. The Blazer had a parking decal, but the lot in front of the Lobo Gymnasium was full. He found a shady place in a visitors' lot in front of a building that bore the name Popejoy Hall. Wales stuck a quarter in the meter and left him to wait.

He used the time to check the map in the glove compartment and look at the registration. It was Wales's vehicle, not Ross Malachy's. Comparing the addresses on Malachy's license with the one on the registration, he deduced that Malachy lived in an apartment at Wales's home. He located the address on the map, and was feeling a little more relaxed when Al popped in again.

"Sam?" The Observer sounded almost furtive.

"Al?" Sam found himself checking out Al's attire to verify which avatar he was talking to. Now that he was face-to-face, or face-to- 'hologram' with his friend again, he could admit to himself that seeing two Als at once was disconcerting to him as well. It was reassuring to have to deal with only one at a time.

"Are you alone?"

Sam made an elaborate show of looking around the parking lot. While not empty, the lot wasn't thickly populated, either. And no one seemed to be interested in a man in a Blazer talking—apparently—to himself.

"I mean, *he's* not here, is he?"

"Wales? No, he went somewhere to drop something off." The moment Sam said the words, he regretted them; Al was in no shape to handle the teasing. "No. You aren't here."

That sounded even worse somehow, but it was the right thing to say. Al glared at him a moment longer. "What the hell are you doing here, Sam?"

"Hey, I thought you were supposed to tell me that."

"You know the rules—you set them up! Observe, that's what we were supposed to do. Not interfere!"

"And somebody changed the rules on us. I Leap, you tell me what I'm supposed to fix, I fix it, and I Leap again. That's the drill—"

"This is different."

The tone of his voice got Sam's complete attention. Al looked like a man about to jump out of his skin. He was shaking worse, if anything, than he had before. He'd left the fedora behind this time, and the threads of silver in his curly dark hair, which should have been glinting in the bright sunlight, were muted in the future, artificial light of the Imaging Chamber, where the Al of whom this was only an image remained. He kept looking around, as if

20

expecting to see his past self jump out at him.

"It's too close," Al went on. "It's too confusing. It's . . . the risk . . . Sam, you *can't* change history this time. You *can't*. If you change anything, maybe I won't—" He stopped himself, actually biting his lip to keep back the words.

Sam stared at him, bewildered. "You won't what?"

Al pulled in a deep breath, swelling out like a cat with puffed fur, and let it go again to shrink into the image of a man even smaller than he really was. "Sam, *think*. You can't change history now. If you do, maybe—"

He stopped, swallowed, went on. "I can't tell you. You have to figure it out for yourself. But it's obvious, isn't it?"

In the silence that stretched between them, Sam looked past the hologram to the blue sky framing the Pueblo Revival architecture of the university buildings, a uniform soft brown and gray with rounded corners. From his current angle he could see a few trees sticking up through the concrete. Somewhere on the other side of Popejoy Hall he thought there was a green park with lots of trees, a pond, and ducks. It might have been some other place, not this one, but it felt right, familiar somehow. Perhaps it was just the feeling of a university, a safe place where people studied and argued and carried on intellectual wars with words and ideas, a good place. He had always liked universities.

"What am I here for this time, Al?" he asked thoughtfully.

He could hear Al's convulsive swallow, see the quick movement of Al's hands out of the corner of his eye. "It's June twenty-second, 1990. You're in

Albuquerque, New Mexico. You could have figured that out for yourself," he added defensively. "I'm not telling you anything."

"No. No, you aren't." Sam smiled to himself, and decided not to tell Al about the newspaper outside the hotel.

A stray blackbird flapped heavily across the parking lot to perch on an iron statue of a wolf, the university's Lobo mascot.

"I wonder what I was doing on June twenty-second, 1990," Sam said. He could feel Al vibrating with tension. "How far along was the Project then . . .?"

"Sam, don't. *Please* don't."

"I'm not changing anything, I'm just wondering. Al, what does Ziggy say I'm supposed to change?"

Silence.

He turned in the seat of the car to look at the other man. "Al, come on. What does Ziggy say?"

Al looked straight back at him and took another deep breath. *He'd better quit that, he's going to hyperventilate*, some part of Sam's mind noted.

"Ziggy isn't sure." Al's fingers around the horse-leg cigar were white with tension. The colored lights blinking in the handlink stuttered, without rhythm. "The thing is, so far, Ziggy doesn't think you're supposed to change anything."

The crow called, sardonic.

"What do you mean, I'm not supposed to change anything? Why would I Leap in here if I didn't have to change something? And if I don't change anything, how can I Leap out again?"

"Ziggy isn't sure you *can* change anything this time," Al said. His voice had even more of a rasp than usual. "The data we have aren't . . .

complete. Right now, Ziggy says there's an eighty-seven-percent chance you're stuck."

The blood drained from Sam's face as the implications sank in. If he was in a situation he couldn't change, he couldn't ever Leap out of it. If he couldn't Leap out . . . he would spend his life as Ross Malachy. He would never be able to go home to his own time and his own body.

"Oh . . . boy," he whispered.

CHAPTER THREE

The apartment was a frame-and-stucco add-on over the garage, with a rickety wooden stairway that led up to the little hideaway. The garage itself projected forward of the house, forming the short leg of an L; he had a view of the yard and the driveway and the front door from the window beside the apartment door. A morning-glory vine twisted and bloomed on the stairway support.

He had a gas stove and a sink and refrigerator in one corner, and a daybed under the window, currently folded back under a bolster and covered with a tattered brown plaid cover, made a couch against the wall.

It was a student's apartment, a serious student's apartment. Two ceiling-high hand-built bookcases were packed solid with textbooks, mostly sociology, some anthropology. He pulled out one loose-leaf notebook and grinned at the title page—*Physics in a Humanist Frame*—and the scrawled notation, "Not enough math to worry you!" It looked like a collection of lectures, printed and distributed by a professor who wasn't sure his audience would stay awake to take notes of their own. Replacing it, he looked around, breathing deeply of the memories of being a student with no greater worries than the next examination, the thesis adviser, the committee. He had always loved school, even when instructors were incompetent and texts incomplete; he had always loved the wonderful process of learning things.

A desk against one wall was Ross Malachy's workplace. On the wall over the desk a tattered poster of Warwick Castle, "Open all the year round except Christmas Day," and a *Playboy* centerfold in somewhat better condition showed that his working habits were subject to distraction. A computer was cast adrift on a sea of notebooks, papers, three-by-five cards, pens and pencils. It drew him like a sea gull to a fishing trawler, and he sprawled down in the kitchen chair before it and turned on the power.

The machine booted directly into a word-processing program he recognized, and he spent the next twenty minutes cruising through Ross Malachy's files, resisting the temptation to add notes to a term paper, feeling like a voyeur reading the young man's love letters to his girlfriend back home in Indiana, his starving-student requests for money from his father, his wiser-older-brother letters to his little sister. Sam remembered writing letters like that to his own little sister, Katie. He couldn't recall what Katie looked like, though.

He shook away the twinge of anger and depression that any reminder of the holes in his memory brought on, and kept on. Reading letters was almost like reading a diary, and was a reprehensible invasion of privacy. But few things could be more of an invasion than the occupation of someone else's body, and Sam had long since resigned himself to the necessity of finding out as much as possible about the people into whose lives he Leaped.

Last fall, Ross had found this apartment. Shortly after that, he had proudly informed his father that he wouldn't be needing quite so much money anymore, as "Dr. Wales is paying me for odd jobs like driving him places." The letter mentioned too that Wales had a wife, and a daughter named Lisa, but offered few details.

The duties, whatever they were, had not interfered with Ross's taking a full class load two semesters in a row, including several graduate-level courses. This summer he was spending more time working for Wales, trying to build up some cash. Sam decided he liked Ross Malachy—he seemed like a prudent, cautious, rather shy kid. Not unlike one Sam Beckett at a similar age.

He glanced at the battered silver watch with the oversize numerals that Ross wore on the inside of his wrist. Almost five o'clock. That would explain the pangs of hunger. His host had a skinny body that required feeding at frequent intervals.

He was exploring the possibilities in the cupboards by the kitchen sink when a knock at the door was followed by its opening. He looked up, startled, to see a girl of perhaps fifteen, with shoulder-length brown hair, too much eye makeup, and uncomfortably tight jeans walk in with no further announcement.

27

"Hello?" Ross must know this girl; her body language said that she didn't expect any surprise at her unconventional entry.

"Hi." Slinging her belt-purse down on the desk as she passed, she elbowed her way past him and opened the refrigerator door, leaning over to inspect the vegetable drawers on the bottom shelf. "You're out of oranges."

Forcing himself to look away from the presentation of her rear end, he cleared his throat. "Uh, yeah, I guess so. Would you like—"

But she had already taken a can of diet ginger ale and was popping the top open. "Boy, it was the pits today."

He closed the refrigerator door behind her as she swaggered over to the threadbare couch and sat sideways on it, balancing the can on her knees, staring at him through lowered lashes.

"It was, huh?" As a conversation starter, it wasn't much. It had the advantage of not committing him to anything, however.

"I thought you said summer school was going to be okay." She rotated the can between her palms. The red of her fingernails and lipstick matched the red on the can exactly. "It's not. It's, like, even worse than regular school. They give *homework*!"

This was evidently such a betrayal that she lapsed into another brooding silence, punctuated only by long, noisy swallows from the can.

"Well, that isn't so bad—" Sam began.

"Stenno says it's a waste of time."

Sam fell silent, waiting for a clue about Stenno. He'd found that if he kept quiet, people would tell

28

him almost everything he needed to know.

It was the "almost" part that kept tripping him up.

"Stenno says they're just jerking me around. I shoulda passed that class." The girl was building up quite a head of steam. "It's not fair. A D was good enough to pass."

"Is 'good enough to pass' really good enough?" Sam asked, curious. He had never in his life received a low grade on anything except flirting.

"But no," she went on, sneering, paying no attention to him, "Daddy says I can do better. So Daddy says I have to take it over. He signed me up without even asking my permission!"

Aha, Sam thought. This must be Wales's daughter, Lisa. Odd, from Ross's letters he'd thought the girl was younger than fifteen. Maybe it was just the difference between Sam Beckett's age and Ross Malachy's.

From outside the garage apartment, he could hear a woman's voice calling, querulous. "Elizabeth? Lizza-bet? Dinner!"

"She *knows* I hate that name," the girl said, as if the woman were deliberately trying to annoy her. Ross had said something about Lisa not liking her real name, Sam recalled. He shrugged. Katie had gone through a stage where she wanted to be called Scholastica. It had lasted exactly twenty minutes, he recalled.

Lisa finished the soft drink, and then a thought occurred to her, and she ducked her head, apologetic. "I was supposed to ask if you wanted to come to dinner."

Sam's—Ross's—stomach growled, and Elizabeth/

Lizza-bet/hated-her-name laughed. "I guess you do, huh? She's making chicken-fried steak."

"Sounds great," Sam said with complete sincerity.

The soft drink can described a perfect arc into a paper sack already half-filled with crushed aluminum cans. "Well, come on, then."

Some ten minutes later Sam was wondering if perhaps he would have been better off scrounging in the apartment refrigerator, or maybe going out foraging for a fast-food hamburger.

The Wales home was a comfortable faux adobe, with false vigas thrusting from the walls at regular intervals. Inside, it was furnished in a mix of Territorial and Sears Best, with pictures of relatives lining the walls of the entryway, Navaho throws over the couch, and a leather recliner in front of the TV set. Every surface was dusted, every knickknack at the best angle for viewing; only the family pictures kept it from feeling more like a model home than a place where real people lived. But even the pictures were studio portraits of Lisa and her parents.

The largest cat Sam had ever seen, a massive brown tabby with the side whiskers of a full-grown lynx, paraded into the dining room, stopped in midstride as it caught sight of him, and paused to clean a foot, making sure in the process that Sam got a good look at a full complement of claws. Weapons polished, it gave him one more glare and stalked off, flicking a haughty, plumed tail in farewell. Sam glanced around again, but couldn't see any cat hair on the furniture. He shook his head wonderingly. Someone was certainly conscientious about cleaning.

"What did you do to Macho?" the girl asked. "Usually he comes right up to you."

"Can't imagine," Sam said. But he knew perfectly well why Macho would reject him. Animals and small children, looking at Ross Malachy now, would see Sam Beckett instead. From time to time he tried to figure out why. Al had said once that it had something to do with brain waves. There were holes in that explanation, but he didn't know whether they were due to Al's lack of scientific expertise or his own scrambled memory.

Al. Al, in two places. He needed to think long and hard about Al. Since Al told him he might be stuck here, he'd been letting his subconscious mull over the problem. He was going to have to give it—them—his full attention. Both problems— why Al was in an encounter group and what he was supposed to change. Because no matter what the Observer said, there had to be something to change in this time line. Otherwise he was going to be stuck as Ross Malachy forever, and Ross Malachy would—

He had no idea what would happen to Malachy between his present moment and Al's. He'd have to ask Al, and hope that that wasn't another one of those things Al didn't want to talk about.

Mrs. Wales was setting a new place at the dining room table for him, putting heavy silver and yellow china on a green place mat. The plate looked like a giant sunflower against a patch of grass.

In the middle of the table an arrangement of dried flowers effectively blocked each person's view of the one sitting opposite. Sam took the platter of breaded meat from the woman and set it on the table, taking the opportunity to nudge the flowers out of dead center.

"Why thank you, Ross." Mrs. Wales was a small woman, with lipstick too red and hair too blonde. She was wearing tan jeans and a black pullover. She was chipper. Very chipper. Almost as if her mood had some artificial help. Sam cast a quick glance around the kitchen as he moved in to take the mashed potatoes, but didn't spot any open liquor bottles. She dodged out of his way, and he reminded himself to give the woman the benefit of the doubt. "You're such a helpful boy!"

"Yeah, suck-up," the girl said under her breath as he passed.

"Lizza-sweet, that was rude."

"Lisa. My name is Lisa. Call me Lisa, dammit!" The girl's voice rose in a shriek. Sam slapped the bowl on the table and turned around to take Lisa's arm, momentarily forgetting that he was a guest, not a big brother. But the expression on the face of the woman standing between himself and the girl stopped him.

For a moment, just a moment, her face looked broken, as if he could see beyond the powder and mascara and lipstick and see someone with faded blue eyes trembling, someone with fragile paper-thin skin stretched over her skull, someone who would be blown away by anger as a leaf would be blown by a hurricane. Another word—any other word—would send her spinning away helplessly. She was watching her daughter with grief and vulnerability.

Lisa saw it too, and was silent. She looked back and forth from her mother to Sam and back again, then spun around and marched away, letting the saloon door of the kitchen flap behind her.

By the time it stilled, Mrs. Wales was moving again, getting serving spoons from the drawer and clicking them together in her hands.

"You know," she said inconsequentially, staring down at the spoons in her hands, "I remember one time, oh it must have been five or six years ago, Lizza—Lisa—came home from school. She was so confused. They'd had a spelling bee that day, and they had the best five spellers from each class, and Lizza was one of the ones from her class. She was the only girl."

The spoons stopped clicking, and her knuckles turned white and red where she grasped them.

"She was the first one to miss a word. And she was so mad, because they said she missed it because she was a girl."

Sam could see tears forming along her eyelashes. "Because she was a girl?" he said softly, prompting her.

"She was the only girl, and she was the first one to miss, so they said it must have been because she was a girl."

He waited, expecting more to the story, but there was no more. The woman sniffed back more tears and fumbled in her pocket for a tissue, setting the spoons down. Sam picked them up as she blew her nose. When she looked up again, she was wearing her mask again.

"Thank you, Ross. If you'll just put those things on the table, I seem to have gotten something on my contact lens. They're such a nuisance, sometimes, contact lenses. It's just vanity, the only reason I wear them. I suppose I think they make me look pretty."

She wasn't fishing for a compliment, he realized, but making up sounds to put between them.

"That's all right," he said, speaking so quickly he stumbled over the words. "You're, you'd look pretty no matter what you—whether you wore contacts or not."

"You are a sweet boy, Ross." She gave him a tremulous smile and left through the other door.

Sam shook his head and took the spoons out to the dining room.

Lisa was sitting at the table, slouched back so that her chin was only inches above the level of the table.

"Do you always scream at your mother?" Sam said, putting the spoons down a great deal more carefully than he wanted to.

Lisa looked slantwise at him through her eyelashes, inhaled as if she were going to say something, and then shook her head, a tiny shake, rejecting her own unspoken comment.

"You know, if my sister had raised her voice that way to my mother—" He paused, trying to imagine first his little sister Katie doing any such thing, and second what would have happened had she done so. The concept was beyond him. He couldn't remember anything like that ever happening.

Which didn't mean that it hadn't. It might have, and his memory simply had a hole where that particular memory was supposed to be. But he could remember flashes of his sister, and of his mother, and the thought of Katie screaming just would not compute. He took a deep breath to explain this at length to the teenager slumped at the table.

"Which story did she tell this time?" Lisa said.

"What?" The question was so unexpected that he had to play it back. "Which story?"

"Yeah." Lisa unfolded herself and sat up straighter in the chair. "She always tells these stories. Like they're some big deal."

"Maybe they are a big deal. She's your mother, after all."

"They're stupid things. *Stupid.* Like one of her favorites is when I learned to tie my shoes. She tells that story like I was some cripple taking her first step."

"She's your mother. Everything a kid does is important to a mother."

"She treats me like a baby!"

"As far as she's concerned, you *are* her baby."

"And am I still going to be a baby when I'm forty?" Lisa said. "When am I going to get to be a grown-up? She can't even call me by my right name, for God's sake!"

"One of the things about being a grown-up, Lisa—" Sam began. The swinging doors opened, and Mrs. Wales came back in, freshly made up. Lisa shot a sneering glance at Sam, who promptly shut up. There would be time for a lecture later, he promised himself grimly.

"Your father is almost through with his meditating, dear. Oh, the table looks so nice! Ross, your mother certainly trained you properly."

"As opposed to the way my mother trained me?" Lisa said.

Her mother flinched and went on gamely. "But you know, you've moved the centerpiece. It's supposed to be in the center of the table. That's why they call it a 'centerpiece,' dear. Let's just shift it back here where

35

it belongs. There, now isn't that so much nicer. So pretty. I do like flowers, don't you? The flowers have been so lovely this year."

"So nice, you mean?" The sarcasm in Lisa's voice could have been cut by a dull butter knife.

Mrs. Wales blinked, and Sam glared at Lisa, mentally adding another chapter to that lecture. The girl had the grace to look faintly ashamed of herself as her mother bustled around the 'nice' table, straightening the place mats, aligning the knives and spoons just so, setting the water glasses exactly in place, filling the salad plates with lettuce and making sure each small plate had a tomato and a carrot slice and a cucumber pleasingly arranged.

Dinner proceeded in a strained silence. Dr. Stephen Wales made a grand progress into the dining room, seated himself, nodded regally to wife, daughter, and Sam, and shook out his napkin. Sam momentarily expected him to take his knife and fork into his fists and transmogrify into Henry VIII, complete with feather in his jeweled cap.

But Stephen Wales remained Stephen Wales, and Lisa remained Lisa, and Mrs. Wales, whose first name Sam still did not know, remained Mrs. Wales. The only one at the dinner table who had transmogrified lately was Ross Malachy, who, unbeknownst to the others present, was really Sam Beckett, time traveler out of joint.

Silver clicked on china. Water sloshed in glasses. There was no coffee. Sam found himself needing the taste of coffee to offset crisply battered chicken-fried steak, mashed potatoes, and peas and carrots, and reminding himself not to ask for bread to cover with gravy. It had been a treat, growing up, to take a piece

36

of his mother's white bread and cover it in brown, salty gravy. It went with this kind of meal, but he could imagine the look on the Waleses' faces. Even his mother had told him that bread-and-gravy was strictly for at-home meals.

It was disorienting, that meal. It tasted like meals he remembered, except for the lack of coffee; the texture and flavor of the food in his mouth were textures and flavors that evoked vivid memories of sunlight flooding through the west window of the kitchen in his parents' house, teasing from his older brother, teasing his younger sister in turn. The teasing never got out of hand. His parents could warn the boys with a glance to mind their manners.

But with this family, there was no teasing, no conversation, even, except "Pass the potatoes, please," and "I'll hand you the pepper, dear, you don't need to reach across for it."

The plates were nearly cleared before Mrs. Wales asked her husband, "Did your meeting go well today, dear?"

"You know we don't discuss the things that go on in the circle, Jennie. Those are men's mysteries."

Sam couldn't keep from rolling his eyes in disbelief. Lisa stifled a giggle and shot him a covert grin.

Wales placed his knife carefully across his plate. "You may find this amusing, young lady, but I assure you it is not. You may not make fun of us."

Sam drew a guilty breath of relief that his own look hadn't been caught by anyone else.

"Oh, I don't have to," Lisa assured her father with a straight face. "You do fine all by yourself."

Wales's brows knitted. "You can't speak to your father that way."

"I'm doing it, aren't I?" she said flippantly, setting her napkin beside her empty plate. Sam had the impression she had done this before, often, and had timed it for the end of the meal on purpose.

"That's enough!"

"Enough of what?" she said, grinning, moving her chair out from the table just enough that she could step away from the table quickly.

Sam shrank into his chair and tried to be invisible. He hoped that whatever he had to do, it wasn't going to be reconciling this father to this daughter. It was beginning to look likely.

From behind him came the sound of the Door sliding open, and he hid a sigh of relief that wasn't guilty at all. Al was back. He wasn't alone in the middle of this warring family any more; he had an ally, even if an invisible one.

After a moment, the Door slid open again, and Al vanished, without comment.

CHAPTER
FOUR

Late in the 1990s, the quantum physicist Sam Beckett would face a crisis on Quantum Leap, a secret project in the New Mexico desert, a few hundred miles from Albuquerque. A skeptical funding agency, unable to follow the obscure mathematics to support his theories about the potential of time travel and appalled at the cost of the computing facility required to support them, demanded to see substantive results immediately, or the project would be closed down. Without consulting his project personnel, he made the last connections and stepped into the glowing blue ring of the Accelerator, hoping, expecting to be able to observe the past within his own life span.

Instead, the past shattered.

Instead of observing the past, he became a part of it.

Somehow, the mathematics and the computer and the experiment threw the essence of Sam Beckett out of his body and into someone else's. The computer, a biomechanical construct named Ziggy, hypothesized that the experiment had jumbled time. In order to get Beckett back—and return the person currently occupying Beckett's body, slumped on the floor of the Imaging Chamber—he had to be located, and the rift healed. They shuffled the body into the Waiting Room, and began searching through time. When the body opened its eyes again, the Project rejoiced. Then they realized that the person who occupied Sam's body wasn't, in fact, Sam.

The only person who could recognize Sam Beckett *as* Sam Beckett was the person who had donated the extra nerve tissue for the neurocells in the hybrid computer: Al Calavicci. By activating Ziggy, that donation had created a resonating link from Al through Ziggy to Sam. Ziggy located Sam in the past by analyzing known history and the concatenation of events necessary to lead to the current— Ziggy's—present. The computer noted that isolated, small events weren't working out the way the data said they ought to, and the lost Dr. Beckett appeared to be drawn to those disruptions. It computed, analyzed, estimated odds, traced the links, and sent Al's image back to help Dr. Beckett return. It helped that they could usually ask the person in Sam's body who he—or she—thought she was.

Unfortunately Dr. Beckett couldn't remember who he was, or who Ziggy was, or what Quantum Leap was. His formerly photographic memory was full of holes. And a frantic Ziggy concluded that to fill the holes would lead to further shattering of the time lines. Sam had to correct some event in the life of the person into whose body he had Leaped in order to return to the restored future, which was Al's present. This much, Al could tell Sam.

The further misfortune, which Al couldn't tell Sam about, was that each time Sam made a correction, other cracks developed. The past, once a seamless whole, now resembled a raku pot pulled out of a furnace. Ziggy couldn't predict where each correction would send Sam next; it could only postulate that the correction had to be made. Otherwise, the present would shatter, instead of simply becoming steadily more warped.

And by this time, the only ones who could remember what the present was *supposed* to look like were Ziggy and Al.

Al couldn't tell Sam anything about his present, the Project poised now at the dawn of a new century, because he didn't know any more than Sam did what it would look like each time Al entered it. So far, it wasn't too different, not in the essentials. All the lines of the future had to have Ziggy; that much they could be reasonably sure of. In all the futures in which Sam Beckett appeared, somehow Project Quantum Leap got off the ground.

However, Al Calavicci wasn't at all sure that *his* presence was required.

He had tried once to imagine what would happen if Sam's mucking around in Time caused him, Al Calavicci, to make some choice that would lead him somewhere else in his life. Would he find himself abruptly somewhere besides the Imaging Chamber, perhaps washing a car some Saturday afternoon outside a house in a residential suburb in Illinois, getting ready to visit the commissary for the week's groceries? Would he find himself suddenly married

41

yet again to a woman who a moment ago he'd never met?

Would he remember the other past, the one wiped out by the change, the way he remembered all the changes Sam had already made?

Up until now it had only been an intellectual exercise, one he played with and discarded hastily at the onset of the inevitable headache. But this time . . . this time it was all too possible.

He could remember the encounter group. He had been in the process of divorcing his fourth, or was it fifth—or—no matter—wife. He was retiring from the Navy. Project Star Bright had wrapped. And the future had seemed awfully bleak. So much so that when the divorce mediator had suggested that as long as he was making one last trip to Albuquerque anyway, he give Stephen Wales's men's self-esteem group a try, he had shrugged and said "Why not?"

For a long moment, Al stood alone in the chilly fluorescent light of the Imaging Chamber, staring down at the oddball collection of colored cubes that was the handlink. It looked like Jujubes melted together in the box, but with lights flashing in irregular patterns inside the little component-boxes.

"Ziggy?" he said. He was pleased, somehow, that his voice was steady. He didn't expect it to be steady.

"Yes, Admiral?" It was a woman's voice, a woman petulant and pampered and spoiled. Al still thought of Ziggy as "he," even though Tina Martinez-O'Farrell, the design engineer who had taken Sam's dream and made it real in metal and plastic, had raised the computer's voice an octave after the last set of problems. Ziggy was experimental. Even Tina

42

didn't understand how the neurocells worked with the rest of the computer design. That meant things went wrong. A lot.

It made for a certain amount of tension on the Project.

So did the fact that every man currently working in the caves and tunnels beneath the New Mexico desert had lustful fantasies about Tina. Including, and perhaps especially, Al Calavicci, who had managed to indulge those fantasies from time to time.

"Is everything . . . still here?"

The following pause might have meant centuries in computing terms, as Ziggy considered the question in terms of what the current state of reality was, compared to what reality had looked like when the Observer had entered the Chamber less than three minutes before.

"Yes, Admiral," Ziggy said at last. "There have been no substantive changes."

Al closed his eyes, suffocating in relief.

"Admiral," the computer went on, "I must remind you that any changes that might be made are not dependent upon your presence, or lack thereof, in Dr. Beckett's current environment. Changes may happen at any time."

"I know that," Al snapped. "I know that."

"The situation is fragile," Ziggy said.

"I know that, too."

"Yes, Admiral." The computer fell silent. The only sound in the Imaging Chamber was the humming from the fluorescent lighting and the air-conditioning that kept the computer cool.

If it weren't for that, Al thought, he could hear his heart beating.

"Okay, open up."

The air-lock door slid up, and Al walked from the buffer zone to the central Control Room, a large space dominated by a version of the handlink that was ten feet long and five feet wide, a multihued table above which a blue-and-silver ball was suspended. The rest of the room was taken up with parts of Ziggy. It took a lot of flash memory to store just over forty years' worth of the world's history.

Gushie, the Project's chief programmer and the man responsible for making sure all that history was available to the computer, was consulting with Tina over a schematic, the two of them oblivious to the technological wonders surrounding them. As Al entered, they looked up, startled.

"That didn't take very long," Tina greeted him. "Is everything, like, okay?"

"Yeah, fine. He's having dinner. We couldn't talk." Al kept going. For a change, he didn't want to savor the view of Tina's long legs and gorgeous body. He failed to see the hurt in her eyes as he stalked past, still thinking about Sam.

He passed the Waiting Room without even glancing at the door; he was in no mood to cope with someone else in Sam Beckett's body today.

What would he do if the telephone in his quarters rang as he walked in the door, and when he picked it up, a stranger's voice said, "Al? It's Sam."

The thought gave him chills. He couldn't imagine what that might mean to the time line. He had comforted himself all along with the thought that Sam had to be back, that the Leaping had to be finished, by the time Ziggy went on-line and Sam's first Leap occurred. Sam couldn't Leap into a time after he

44

started Leaping. Or so Al had always thought.

Apparently he was wrong.

He wasn't up to the mathematics of it. He was a jet jock, not a physicist.

The door to his quarters looked exactly like all the other doors along the housing corridor. He reached for the printplate to release the door lock, and paused. What if it was different? What if the time line had changed, and things weren't where they were supposed to be?

That way lay madness. He jerked his head in negation and slapped his hand against the sensor surface, and the door opened.

Everything was the same. Still the dull cream-colored walls, the barren room with bed and desk and terminal and—blessedly silent—telephone. Al Calavicci traveled light, didn't decorate. The two posters on the wall were standard issue, not of his choosing, and he couldn't tell you what they were if he wasn't looking at them.

The sight of Sam, sitting at the Waleses' table, eating dinner, had somehow been the very last straw. He had been chasing Sam through time for years now. The only break he ever got was between Leaps, while Ziggy tried to figure out when Sam had gone now, and they never knew how long it would take to pin him down or what kind of situation he'd be in. He was *tired*.

And if he was tired, Sam had to be that much more so; from his perspective Leaps were simultaneous. He barely solved one situation when he was dropped into another, generally under the most dangerous or embarrassing conditions possible.

Chicken-fried steak, however, was neither dangerous nor embarrassing, and Ziggy couldn't figure out what Sam could change without drastically affecting matters. It was time to leave well enough alone.

The electronic cough that was Ziggy being diffident made him jump. Sam had programmed the computer not to break a long silence without some warning. The warning was as bad as the stream of data that Ziggy used to launch into before.

Now, at least, the computer waited for an acknowledgment.

"Yeah, what is it?"

"You still retain the handlink, Admiral."

"So?" He was feeling churlish. Sam used to be able to talk him out of this mood.

Maybe Sam *was* talking him out of this mood, right this minute. A chill traced delicately down his spine.

"Gushie would like to examine this component, Admiral."

No. Sam wasn't talking him out of anything. He was having dinner with the Wales family.

Or perhaps not, since time seemed to pass differently for Sam while Leaping than for the people who tried to keep track of him.

"Tell Gushie . . . tell Gushie I'll drop it off on my way out."

"Are you going somewhere, Admiral?"

"Yeah. I'm going to LA and catch a hockey game."

A pause.

"We will be unable to remain in touch with Dr. Beckett if you're gone, Admiral." The computer's voice was strained. Al told himself that it was only his imagination. Ziggy was only a computer, after

46

all. Or had been the last time he looked.

"He's doing fine all by himself." The Observer pulled a small briefcase from under the bed and began packing in efficient Navy style. "Sam doesn't need me in this one."

"I don't agree," Ziggy responded.

"Tough." He slapped his shaving kit in on top of the neatly folded shirts.

"Dr. Beckett wouldn't abandon you."

Al flinched, but kept on packing.

The computer held its peace.

He finished packing and headed out the door. Ziggy remained silent.

CHAPTER

FIVE

Contrary to Al's belief, Sam felt he could have used all the help he could get. The conversation between Lisa and her father had stalled out, and dinner was coming to a close in an echoing silence. Silverware clattered against the heavy yellow china plates. Mrs. Wales kept sneaking glances at her husband and daughter as if she wanted to say something but couldn't decide what; her husband, for his part, made a show of enjoying his food and ignoring everyone else. Lisa pushed potatoes around the plate and ate nothing at all. Sam wondered if she might not be anorexic, but she looked too healthy for that.

He wanted to know what was going on with this family. Was Mrs. Wales an alcoholic, or sick? Was Lisa flunking summer school? What?

And why was Al in Albuquerque, anyway? Shouldn't he be in Washington, D.C.?

Jenniver Wales had barely swallowed the last bite of peas and carrots when she was on her feet, bringing in the dessert, an old-fashioned Apple Brown Betty. Lisa put a resounding period to the idea of being an anorexic by reaching for a large helping with every indication of eagerness. Wales broke his self-absorbed silence to say, "Put that back."

"What?" The girl was so startled that she dropped the spoon. Apples and cinnamon smeared the table.

"Oh now look what you've done," her mother began, but her husband interrupted.

"If you can't eat dinner with the rest of us, you certainly can't have any dessert, young lady."

"Oh, come on, Dad, I'm not six years old!"

"Then stop behaving that way."

"Oh for God's sake," Lisa snapped, getting up.

"Sit down."

Sam had heard Army generals with less authority in their voices. Lisa froze in place, half sitting, half standing, staring at her father in disbelief.

"Sit *down*." His hands were resting on the table, consciously loose.

Lisa straightened up. "I have to meet Stenno," she said, her voice very small at first, but getting stronger as she got to the name.

"I told you to do something," her father said.

"And I'm telling you to go to hell," Lisa answered.

"If you leave this house, don't expect to come back."

"Who says I'd want to?" And Lisa walked out the door, leaving her father staring after her, her mother weeping quietly into the forgotten Apple Brown Betty.

And Sam thought with a sinking sensation that he knew the problem to be solved this time.

Wales looked after his daughter, baffled, shredding his napkin, and then glared at Sam and his wife, as if daring them to say anything. When they were silent, he got up, stumbling a little over the leg of his chair.

"Ross, I want to see you in the library, please."

It really was a library, much to Sam's surprise; the room had probably originally been a bedroom, but three walls were invisible behind solidly packed floor-to-ceiling bookshelves. The fourth wall had originally been the closet. The sliding doors had been removed, and the cubbyhole revealed was filled with filing cabinets.

The functional walnut desk held a more up-to-date computer than Ross Malachy's, and a mismatched table beside it supported a laser printer and several stacks of paper.

"I don't know what to do with her," Wales said. He sounded tired and hopeless. "I just don't know. She's going out with that damned gangster, and she won't listen. I try and I try, and she won't listen." He fell into the office chair. His face was furrowed with anxiety. "Don't ever have daughters, Ross. They don't listen."

"Well . . ." *Gangster?* Sam thought, startled. Not many people used the word *gangster* anymore, not for kids. Not even members of a gang. *Gang members,* that was the term. In a way it was a shame; "gangster" had so much more flavor. It called up images of wide lapels and snap-brim fedoras and narrow ties— no, that was Al. Well, if you gave Al a tommy gun, he could pass for a gangster, Sam supposed.

Wales was still talking, and Sam forced himself to pay attention.

"They don't listen. Women don't listen. That's why it's so important." Like a man who has caught sight of a lifeline, energy returned to Stephen Wales. "It's *important* that men learn to return to their essential masculinity. We cannot expect respect from our women unless we learn to respect ourselves."

Sam winced. "They're not possessions," he pointed out.

"What? Who?" Wales paused in the process of shuffling through a mound of paper, peered at him myopically through the thick glasses.

"Women. You said '*our* women.' They're not ours. They're people too."

Wales smiled in a condescending fashion. "When you're married, you'll understand, Ross. Of course we don't think of them as mere possessions."

Of course not. Not "mere." But their meaning was only in relationship to him, all the same. Wife, daughter, house, planets revolving around the sun that was Stephen Wales.

"But that's not important. We're going to have another circle tomorrow night; I want you to make sure that the hotel has coffee available, and that we can set up well ahead of time. If they can't provide the simplest amenities for our group, we'll just have to find another place to meet. I want you to look into that, too. See if we can find someplace a little cheaper." He pulled out a receipt, switched on the computer, muttered to himself as it booted directly into a spreadsheet program.

"What about Lisa?" Sam asked.

"Lisa? I'll take care of Lisa. I told her what I would do, and I'm going to do it."

Sam replayed the dinner-table conversation in his mind. "You said she didn't have to come back. . . ."

"I said what I said." Wales closed his eyes briefly, took a deep breath. "A real man doesn't back down. If she's going to live under my roof, she has to live by my rules. That's one of the tough things about being a man, Ross. You can't allow that weakness, that wavering back and forth trying to please everyone, that vacillation, to overcome you. Each one of us has to reach inside himself to his essential maleness and find the primitive strength to establish and maintain his will over his own place, his own territory. What a real man says, *is*. If Lisa realizes that I mean what I say, it will provide her with the sense of security she needs. A parent has to provide limits and boundaries."

Sam looked at the man who was half-sprawled in the chair, peering through thick glasses at the computer screen, poking at the keyboard, talking about essential maleness. There was nothing in the picture that necessarily contradicted the notion of essential maleness, but Stephen Wales's attitude didn't reinforce it, somehow, speeches notwithstanding. He was an overweight, bald, nearsighted man in his early sixties making brave talk about strength and will and place. It should have been pathetic.

It wasn't, somehow.

"What does that mean for Lisa?" he asked.

"If Lisa rejects my rules, she can't expect my roof over her head. I don't wish to discuss this any more, Ross. Please check with the hotels, and I'd appreciate it if you'd look at that faucet in the back bathroom.

53

Jenniver says it's been dripping again."

"Yes, sir."

Jenniver Wales set the dishes in the stainless steel sink very slowly, very carefully, so that the china wouldn't make a noise against the metal. She was breathing through her lips, controlling the rate and volume of each breath so that no one could accuse her of panting. She had done that when Lizza—when Lisa was born, too, refusing to pant even at the urging of the doctors. The indignity of giving birth was bad enough without allowing oneself to breathe in a disgustingly audible manner.

The doctors said that panting would help the pain of labor, but she'd chosen to endure it instead, holding on to a stoic vision. Perhaps it would help the pain she was feeling now, too. She might give it a try. Glancing over her shoulder toward the dining room, she decided against it. Someone might come in.

Besides, this pain wasn't anything like the pain of giving birth. This pain came and went, and for long periods, hours sometimes, it didn't hurt at all, and she didn't have to think about her breathing. When it did come, it came suddenly, like talons sinking into her guts, clenching and twisting, squeezing and yanking her intestines, and she had to hold very still to keep control, to keep from screaming and maybe even passing out. She hoped that no one noticed her abruptly closed eyes and the hunching over, as if to shelter the agony. She couldn't help it, though she tried.

Stephen would be upset with her if she passed out.

Stephen was so easily upset lately. She forced herself to think about Stephen, and as the pain eased she straightened up again. It was too bad of—Lisa—to argue with her father that way. Why, Jenniver's father would no more have tolerated such back talk than he would have grown wings to fly. Stephen was right, Lisa ought to respect her father more. He only wanted what was best for her.

And he shouldn't have to explain his decisions. Lisa was still a child, after all. The decisions were there to be followed, and that was all there was to it. If she'd just do as she was told, there wouldn't be the need for all this fighting all the time.

She scraped the remains of the potatoes into the disposal and ran water over the plates, watching the gravy thin and disappear. Nobody had eaten much, not even Stephen. Usually Stephen ate everything and asked for seconds. He liked her cooking. He liked the way she kept house, too, even if he never said so. And he was a good man. He tried so hard to live up to his ideals.

Of course, anybody would lose their appetite over a scene like the one this evening. She'd have to remember to tell Lisa that. It would be her fault if Stephen woke hungry in the middle of the night. That was an unkindness the child probably didn't even realize she was doing. She needed to be told. A person's actions affected a lot of things, more than you'd think at first. It was hard for a young person to understand that.

Sighing, she blew a stray thread of hair out of her face. She needed to sew a button on that pink blouse or she couldn't wear it to the store tomorrow. If she looked right, maybe Sandra would let her work the counter instead of stocking shelves all day. It was interesting, knowing all the things that a drugstore had, but it wasn't very challenging.

Plates into the dishwasher, silver washed by hand and patted dry. No spots on Mother Wales's good silver!

The roses needed trimming. The early blooms were gone by now. She could get a good couple of hours' work in the garden. That would be wonderful; she could work some new sand into that corner, get rid of some of those weeds. It was restful, turning over the earth, kneeling on the little blue plastic pad and digging deep, planting seeds, checking the sprinkler system, knowing all those green things were there because she, Jenniver Wales, had put them there. Such a responsible, happy feeling. If you did everything right, the seeds grew every time, and with seeds, you could know just about all the right things to do ahead of time. The garden was her favorite place of all.

Stephen and Lisa never came out into the garden.

"Mrs. Wales?"

The voice startled her, and she almost dropped one of the water glasses when she spun around. Ross was standing in the kitchen doorway. He looked properly apologetic.

"I'm sorry, I didn't mean to scare you."

"Oh, it was nothing," she assured him. "Nothing at all."

He was looking at her so intently, though, that she mentally tagged the words a fib. Ross's eyes were that intense Irish blue, and he had sharp features that looked shockingly pale under that thatch of black hair. Black Irish, he'd told her when they first met.

But now he was looking at her almost like her doctor did when she went in for her last checkup. She almost expected the boy to put his hands around her neck to feel her glands, and tilt back her head to examine her eyes. It was concentrated and impersonal at the same time, and she decided that she didn't like it, not one bit. Ross had no right and no reason to be looking at her in that fashion.

So her next words were sharper than usual. "Can I help you with something, Ross?"

He blinked, somewhat abashed. But the intentness didn't go all the way away. "Are you all right, Mrs. Wales?"

"Of course I'm all right. What a thing to say!" She snapped the tea towel and turned back to the sink, hoping that the nervousness didn't show. What a state of affairs, to have a student boarder ask a personal question like that.

But at least he noticed, a small voice in the back of her mind pointed out.

"I'm sorry. I thought you looked a little tired."

"Well, it isn't easy being a two-career woman, you know," she said, deliberately lightening her tone. "Work and home. Home and work!"

"Can I help you with that?" he said, moving beside her to take the aluminum pan that had held the remains of the chicken-fried steak. "I can wrap that up—"

"Don't you be silly, that's my job." She opened her mouth to continue, to suggest that he bring in the other dishes from the table, when the pain seized her again between one breath and the next, and she was held frozen. *Don't pant. Don't make a noise.*

Don't scream.

"Are you sure you're all right?"

There, the silly boy had his hand underneath her arm, was trying to get her attention. *Don't talk to me,* she wanted to say to him. *Can't you see I need all my energy to keep from screaming? I can't spend any listening to you talking. Don't talk to me. Don't talk to me.*

Don't talk to me.

CHAPTER

SIX

He thought he could remember seeing that look before, the inner-directed look of stillness of someone regarding her own pain, afraid to move lest it be awakened and overcome the watcher, afraid to jostle a contained agony because the thin skin of self-control might break and send it soaking through the whole body. His brother had said once, looking down at a splinter of bone sticking up through the skin of his own right arm, "No, it doesn't hurt. The pain is down there. It's not up here with me."

He could see, too, the first hesitant movement that said, "The pain is going away . . . isn't it?" and the cautious sigh of relief that probed the depths of the body and reported back, "The pain is gone. Yes. Gone. Safe. I'm safe now."

"Mrs. Wales, are you all right?"

She resisted his efforts to guide her to a chair, looking pointedly at his hand until he let go of her arm.

"I'm quite all right, Ross, thank you for asking." Her voice was still thready, but gaining strength with every pause between the words.

"You look—have you seen a doctor?"

"Ross, I appreciate your interest in my welfare, but it really isn't your concern. There is nothing the matter with me. Nothing at all. Please don't mention it again."

Color was coming back into her face. It was almost possible to believe her. She pushed a wisp of hair back into place. "Now, was there something you wanted?"

He could push, or he could back away; her attitude said that nothing was the matter, really, he had been mistaken. He chose to back away. For the time being.

"I was looking for a wrench. Dr. Wales said you had a leaky faucet in the back bathroom. All it needs is a new washer. If you've got a wrench—"

"Well, where did you put it?" she asked reasonably. "You were the one who had it last."

For a split second he could hear his own mother saying the same thing, as if two separate images of Jenniver Wales and Thelma Beckett had fused into one matronly woman giving him a universal Mother look. He opened his mouth to replay and shut it again, knowing when he was outclassed.

"I, uh, I don't remember."

"How do you expect to be able to keep track of things if you don't put them back where they belong? Did you look in the toolbox?"

"Well . . ." *I would if I knew where the toolbox was,* he thought frantically.

"Go look in the garage. Shoo." She flapped the towel at him, and he ducked out of the kitchen and picked the most likely door for the garage.

Like most garages in Albuquerque, this one had never housed a car. The cement floor was innocent of any oil stains. Against the house-side wall, at once taking advantage of and providing greater insulation, a freezer, washer, and dryer stood. Opposite, a pegboard hung against the wall, holding rakes and shovels and shears and hoes and other implements of gardening, lined up by size and silently eager to dig into the earth, lop off dead branches, prune and plant and make Nature organized. Sacks of sand and fertilizer and manure, some part used and some new and unopened, waited beneath, already loaded into a child's red wagon.

Between machinery and gardening implements, taking up the center of the garage, was a table holding an unwieldy pile of tools and machinery. Some of the tools had been jostled off the table and kicked underneath, half hiding a large red-painted metal toolbox. It looked as though Mrs. Wales had occasion to remark about neatness fairly often.

The box had been pushed deep, but there was nothing in the way; he hauled it out again and opened it up, picking through the jumble of screwdrivers and nails and files.

Finally, exasperated, he upended the box and started sorting. Shelves against a third wall yielded small jars for the assortment of nails and screws and washers; by the time he finished, he had three wrenches and a stack of other hand tools, including a broken saw.

Replacing the tools in some kind of order took another few minutes, and then the only place for the box was back under the table.

"Maybe I'm here to clean the garage," he murmured.

But there was no sound of a Door opening, no Al to pop through and assure him that yes, indeed, there was a 98-percent chance that he was here to clean up the Waleses' garage, and once it was neat and tidy he would Leap again.

He held his breath, hoping that Al would show up any second. But even when he had to let the breath go, Al had still not appeared, and he sighed and picked up the wrench and set out to tackle the dripping faucet in the back bathroom.

It was a tiny room, cramped with the sink and the commode and the tub. A small window let in the evening breeze, cooling the June heat. The bathroom was done in pastel blues and greens, and the shower curtain and the window curtain matched, with two-dimensional angelfish swimming through sea fronds. The floor was a matching blue tile. It was enough to make him wish for an oxygen tank.

He opened up the cabinet under the sink and twisted himself around to see what was in it. The space between the sink and the tub was barely eighteen inches wide, and it was an awkward fit, even in Malachy's slender body. He had to shift a plastic bucket filled with scrub brushes, a paper sack with dried-out sponges, and a glass jar containing slivers of soap to find a shallow pan catching the water welling up from the joint.

The curtain at the window fluttered and settled again.

He wiggled out from under the sink and looked for the valve to turn the water off. It wasn't immediately visible; he had to haul everything out of the cabinet to find it, and then struggle to get it turned.

Hoping that he had turned the water valve the right way, he set the wrench, propped his feet against the tub, and braced himself to heave.

"Hey, baby."

The voice was so close that he stopped in mid-grunt. Al? It sounded like Al; the noises that followed the greeting sounded like Al, too. But Al was a hologram; he couldn't actually touch anything in this time. . . .

But there was a real Al in this time too.

Sam scrambled back to his feet.

"Hey, hey, glad to see me? You have trouble getting out?"

It wasn't Al. Through the window he could see a blond head bending over Lisa. He couldn't see much else, but he could imagine where the blond's hands were. He stepped back and almost fell over the toilet trying to get out of Lisa's line of sight. It was an excruciatingly uncomfortable situation.

"He threw me out," Lisa said when she came up for air. "He doesn't want me to see you, Stenno." She sounded much less sure of herself than she had when she was baiting her father at the dinner table. Part of it was due to breathlessness, no doubt, but that still left some uncertainty unaccounted for.

"Bastard," the boy said. "You don't need him. You got me, baby. You and me are going to have lots and lots of money."

63

He kissed her again. Sam waited, brows knit, but the two moved away, and a moment later he heard the roaring of an engine.

So this was Stenno, the boyfriend that Lisa had to meet. Sam took a deep breath. From not seeing anything to change, crises were suddenly erupting out of the woodwork: Stephen Wales couldn't get along with his daughter, Jenniver Wales was obviously suffering from some medical problem, and now Stenno was talking about having lots and lots of money.

And then there was Al, too; what was Al doing in Albuquerque, and why was he attending an encounter group? Al was a skeptic through and through, and Sam would have bet the fillings out of his teeth that the feisty former Admiral would be the last man in the world to be half-naked in a room full of other half-naked men, shuffling in a circle and chanting to the syncopated beat of a drum. If there was ever a man certain of his masculinity, it was Al Calavicci.

And that same Al Calavicci, Sam's Al from the future, the hologrammatic Observer, insisted that there was nothing here to change, that everything had to be left strictly alone. And then he disappeared.

And unlike all the other times, Al hadn't come back.

Sam felt very much on his own.

CHAPTER

SEVEN

Al Calavicci sat alone in a hotel room, feet up on a small round table, smoking the biggest cigar he could find, and peered narrowly through the resultant haze of smoke at—nothing.

The room was decorated in Pueblo Deco, with an imitation R. C. Gorman print over the dresser and walls that were painted brown and orange, presumably to evoke thoughts of a desert sunset. The bedspread was gray and black and brown and cream, reminiscent of a Navajo rug; the carpet was standard hotel-room mustard yellow. Everything was faded out by years of dust and wear. It wasn't what he would have chosen, if he'd had his choice; the per diem the military offered even an admiral on temporary duty was barely enough to cover the cost of the room and one decent meal in the hotel restaurant.

Resting on the table next to his spit-polished shoes was a letter. In precise, dry lawyerly fashion it informed him that his fifth wife's petition for the dissolution of their marriage would be heard, and therefore, and in consequence. . . .

Al knew the consequences. He'd been through it all before, several times. He could go through a divorce in his sleep, he sometimes thought.

In the briefcase at his feet were other documents, notifying him of the time and place of his retirement from the United States Navy. The assignment that brought him to Albuquerque, meetings with the Labs about the design of a new pressure switch, would be the last one.

And a letter from the man he considered his best friend, inviting him to help celebrate. Sam had finally got some funding for that crazy project of his, but the government slapped security restrictions on it at the same time, so now he could only hint broadly and refer to their late-night conversations when they'd both been working on Star Bright. Nothing could hide the excitement Beckett felt, though. He was filled with delight and terror and determination to rip history open for his inspection.

And at the same time, because Sam Beckett was smart—he was the smartest guy Al had ever met, at least as far as academic things went—he already knew what he wouldn't do. Time was fragile, he'd told Al once. The two of them sitting in that officers' club, drinking by God ginger ale—the memory made him wince, even to consider it, but Sam wouldn't let him touch alcohol then—talked about how even as that moment was *their* present, it was also the past for the two of them in the future.

It was like skating along a Möbius strip. He didn't get it then, and he couldn't begin to follow the math that the younger man, in his enthusiasm, began to scribble all over the tablecloth. Sam knew that this project was what he was born for. Al had envied him then.

He envied him now. Off in the desert, building some computer the likes of which had never been even thought of before, wholly committed body and soul and formidable intellect to a project fabulous both literally and figuratively, caught up in the beginning of the rest of his life—

While he, Al Calavicci, sat in a hotel room and contemplated the endings that were all arriving at once.

He was resilient. He hadn't survived years as a POW because he was a quitter. So his marriage was over, and he had no family—he could always get married again. There were lots of luscious lovely ladies out there.

But it was a hell of a time to be retiring—things were so damned unsettled in the USSR, and there was that madman in the Middle East. He blew a smoke ring at the ceiling, picturing it as a frame for the Madman du Jour.

In a life full of craziness, the military was a safe place. You wouldn't think so in the cockpit of a fighter, and you sure as hell wouldn't think so when the plane went down, but it was. You always had a job to do and a reason to get up in the morning; you always had a place—okay, maybe you spent too much time in the Club and Bachelor Officers Quarters, and it was never going to be fancy, not on military pay—but it was a place and a status and a hospital when you were sick.

And you felt needed. Except, well, maybe after 'Nam he didn't feel needed so much. He'd thought Beth would still be waiting for him. But there were other women out there, and he'd found another one quickly enough. And another. And another. . . . They were wonderful creatures, women. But they always went away, eventually, and you didn't feel like they really *needed* you.

Kind of like now, in fact.

His face twisted at the thought, and he locked it away.

Then there was this business with Wales. Male bonding. Essential masculinity. Getting in touch with your feelings—talk about crazy. Al Calavicci always knew what his feelings were, especially when it came to the ladies, and if that wasn't essential masculinity, what was? But standing around in a circle with your shirt off, grunting, chanting to the sound of a drum—crazy. As if that stuff would do any good.

But just for a minute there it felt, kinda—

Well, maybe he'd go back one more time. Just once, to see what was going on. He'd promised the divorce mediator that he'd give it a fair shot. Now it looked like Rita wasn't going to wait and see if chanting would improve their marriage. She was pushing for an immediate dissolution. Al smiled wryly to himself. It had probably been easier to make up her mind with him out of town. So he could quit if he wanted to.

But he still had a week of talking to the engineers, and he had to keep himself busy somehow, and he didn't feel much like finding extracurricular entertainment. It wasn't a good move anyway when the property settlement was still under discussion.

Perhaps he should stick with Wales and his grunt group for a few more meetings.

Besides, he had a little mystery to solve, to figure out why that kid—what was his name, Ross—who helped out Wales, seemed so damn familiar all of a sudden. He knew he'd never seen the boy before signing up for this group-encounter stuff, yet for a split second it was as if he'd known him for years.

It wasn't as if he had anything better to do for the next week. So he'd go back, just to see.

Couldn't hurt.

Al Calavicci, ex-Admiral, sprawled bare-chested on a chaise longue beside a heated swimming pool, chewing fiercely on an unlit cigar, and peered over very dark sunglasses at the few long-stemmed lovelies who were braving the December chill to do laps. Whenever one of them caught him at it he hastily shoved the glasses back up on his nose and made a show of stretching to look up at the sky.

He liked the athletic type. These ladies definitely knew how to take care of their bodies. He was willing to bet they knew how to take care of his body, too. The only question was, which one would he pick, if he had to pick just one? That blonde was lovely. Elegant. And that bikini, that was a work of art. But there was the taller brunette, and he did have a weakness for tall brunettes. Most of his ex-wives were tall brunettes. Taller than he was, anyway.

The fact that this was not necessarily a difficult criterion to meet didn't bother him in the least.

"Mr. Calavicci?"

Al glanced up, startled, to see one of the hotel staff standing by, shaking in the wind. The kid was wearing a nifty little outfit with a jacket, and it was still too cold. Al supposed that some people had a higher heat threshold than others, but surely, in Las Vegas even December couldn't be cold enough to make a normal person shiver, could it? "Huh?"

"You have a call, Mr. Calavicci." The bellgirl shoved a vuphone in his face and beat it back inside the casino.

"Oh." Al sneaked a glance at the swimmers to see if they were impressed, but the last one was getting out of the pool and wrapping herself in an entirely too bulky towel, swaying her way to the entrance that led to the hotel part of the complex. With a snort that would have looked suspiciously like a pout if anyone had been around to see it, Al flipped open the lid. "Hello?"

"Al?" The image in the tiny screen was a little fuzzy, but he could still see her jaws moving as she masticated a wad of bubble gum. "Al, honey, are you there?"

If Al hadn't seen, first, a copy of Tina Martinez-O'Farrell's IQ scores, and second, the transformation that occurred when she got deep into the guts of computer design, he would have considered her an airhead of the highest order. Since she was also gorgeous, this was not necessarily a disadvantage. The fact that she *was* the second smartest person he'd ever met was an added fillip. Now if she'd only lose the gum.

But she always chewed when she was anxious, and judging by the size of the bubbles, she was having a major attack. Al shifted his cigar from one corner of his mouth to the other and heaved a quiet sigh. It wasn't as if he hadn't seen this coming.

70

"See, I *told* you he'd be in Vegas," she said to someone off screen. A confusion of voices temporarily overcame the pickup, and it shrieked in electronic protest.

"Sounds just like the damned handlink," Al muttered. A cloud drifted over, casting a shadow over the pool, and the hairs on his chest stirred and lifted, responding to the drop in temperature. On the other side of the pool, a couple huddled deep in overcoats hurried past, sending incredulous looks his way. "Wimps," he sneered. The wind began to thresh the tops of the palm trees.

The phone squawked again, cleared its throat, and Tina said, "Al, you gotta come back!"

The gain began to climb again, and she turned to shush the others behind her. "Al, you gotta come back. Ziggy says—"

"I don't care what Ziggy says," he said firmly. "I'm not coming back."

He could see Tina's mouth moving, but the words coming from the tiny speaker were something else entirely.

"Admiral Calavicci, it is imperative that you return to the Project."

The voice was pleasant, warm, feminine, and the product of a complex neuromechanical assembly buried deep in a mostly artificial New Mexican cave. It sounded as if it ought to belong to someone tall and lovely and lots of fun on a date. Al was not deceived. He had never had fun with Ziggy. Not ever. And he wouldn't have dated it if it were the last biocomputer in the world.

Which it probably was, come to think of it. Or at least, Ziggy was the first biocomputer in the world, and probably the only biocomputer in the world. He hoped.

"Go to hell," he answered.

"Not practical at the present time," Ziggy responded, unperturbed. "I repeat, it is essential that you return. Additional information has become available relating to Dr. Beckett's current . . . situation."

Al glared, getting out of the chaise longue and shrugging on a purple-and-pink terry-cloth robe. He had to set down the phone to tie the belt, and Ziggy raised its voice. "Admiral, plane reservations have been made in your name on a flight ETD McCarran at sixteen hundred hours."

"Do you mind? I'm a civilian now. Speak civilian. Or if you can't speak civilian, at least speak good Navy. Sixteen hundred hours, my eye." He slipped on a pair of large fuzzy slippers, totally inappropriate for poolside wear, and took one last sip out of his glass of ginger ale.

Sam Beckett had programmed Ziggy to demonstrate a number of human characteristics. Infinitely patient sighs were among them. "The plane leaves at four in the afternoon. In two hours. You have time to pack. I have contacted the concierge and settled your bill. There are seven taxis presently available at the front door, three of which are from licensed cab companies. The ticket will be waiting for you at Gate C-Two. You will, of course, be carrying your luggage on board."

"Of course. You're worse than a yeoman," he muttered.

Ziggy was also fitted with extremely acute acoustic sensors. "Efficiency is considered a valuable attribute in a yeoman, Admiral."

"Look, I don't think I should go back there." By this time he was flopping through the casino area, stepping around the slot-machine banks, dodging the change girls. Someone hit a royal flush, and the jackpot bells and whistles and whirling lights went off.

"The casino route does not lead to your hotel room," Ziggy shouted.

"Hah. A lot you know."

"I contain the floor plans of all the major Las Vegas hotel casinos in my main memory."

"Why did Sam program that?" By this time he was into the poker area, which was considerably quieter.

"Dr. Beckett's motives are unknown. However, given the proclivities of his administrative manager, I would conjecture that he envisioned that a situation such as the one actualized might someday occur. Dr. Beckett could be remarkably prescient. It was a characteristic of his to foresee possibil——"

"Stop talking about him like he was dead," Al snapped. He left the casino and began walking down the mall alley. The hallway was lined on either side with small, expensive shops filled with jewels, faux furs, and My Parents Went to Las Vegas and All I Got Was This Crummy T-Shirt. One display contained a small pink mechanical pig that spun in its open box, snorted three times through a very flexible nose, and spun again. Al broke stride to watch it, feeling a certain fellowship as it spun again, going nowhere.

"Dr. Beckett had a knack for predicting future events," Ziggy said. "From data received, I conjecture that you are now standing outside the souvenir shop which stands at the east end. . . ."

73

"I told you, quit using the past tense. He's not dead."

"But he isn't here, either," Ziggy pointed out. "And without your assistance, Admiral, it is unlikely that he will ever be able to return to his proper time.

"You can't run out on him, Admiral."

The pig spun and grunted, nose wiggling.

"I'm not running out on him. He's just . . . he's too close." A pair of children running past looked at him and giggled at the sight of the man in the purple-and-pink robe and matching purple swim trunks who stood talking into the vuphone. He shrugged and went on down the hall.

"Dr. Beckett's physical and temporal location does not appear to be relevant to the Leap process, so long as he remains within the theoretical parameters established by the theory. He is certainly well within the span of his own lifetime."

"He's *too close,*" Al insisted. He was in the hotel complex now, waiting for an elevator. A herd of Japanese tourists filed out of the next car to arrive, and he entered it and slumped against the mirrored wall.

"He's too close," Al went on, as the doors slid shut and the elevator began to rise. "Ziggy, you know— Ziggy, can the others hear us?"

"No, Admiral. They have left the room."

"Good." Al closed his eyes. "Ziggy, you know how many things have changed. That's what he's *doing,* changing things! That's why he Leaps, to change things."

"So far as we know," the computer noted pedantically.

74

"So far as we know, my left foot. The only way he can Leap is to change something. And we've seen what happens. You and I know the things that aren't the way they used to be. Hell, I watched the head of a Senate committee change sex as a result of a Leap. But we want it to happen, don't we? To make enough changes to get him back?"

"Theoretically, the cumulative changes should be self-correcting, so that eventually Dr. Beckett will return to his own body." There was a small hum. "The senator did not actually change sex, Admiral. The identity of the senator in question changed as a result of Dr. Beckett's actions."

"Yeah, yeah. Details. It was a man who didn't want to fund us, and then a second later it was a woman who gave us another chance. Same difference." The elevator doors opened, and Al flopped out and down the hall, chewing fiercely on his cigar. The vuphone remained silent, showing an unchanging scene of blinking lights, pink and green and yellow. As he approached the door to his room, he raised his hand for the beam to scan his palm, and the lock released.

The maid had already been in, the bed was made, the curtains were open. A small black suitcase was half-hidden behind a table; that and a garment bag in the closet were the only signs that the occupant of the room hadn't already checked out.

Al dropped the vuphone on the stacked pillows and began to pace up and down the room, slippers flopping with every step.

"The thing is," Al said, "every time he changes something so he can get back, things change for us, too. Mostly little things, sure, but—" He was waving his arms wildly by this time— "The part that bothers me is, what if what he changes this time—"

"Causes you to decide against joining the Project?" the computer interrupted.

"Yeah." Al tried to laugh. "That's silly though, isn't it? I mean, if I had decided not to join the Project, I'd—I wouldn't be here, would I?"

"That's correct, Admiral." There was a weight of foreboding in the artificial voice.

Al stopped in mid-turn and stared at the tiny screen. "What would happen to me?"

Ziggy took a long moment to respond. "There are several possibilities, Admiral. . . ."

"Like what?" The general air of silliness was gone, even though the slippers remained. Now the man in the purple-and-pink swim trunks and matching terry-cloth robe was an Admiral again.

The computer was still hesitant. "A number of scenarios present themselves. . . ."

"Cut the crap, Ziggy. What's the top one, and what are the odds?"

Ziggy cleared its mechanical throat, another habit Sam had programmed "for when he has bad news."

"The odds favor a scenario in which you decide to pursue a career in a research-and-development organization in Washington, D.C."

"But I haven't decided that yet."

"No." There was no hesitancy at all in that answer.

"How can you tell?" Al asked. "If I'm not there with Sam, monitoring the situation?"

"As you conjectured, Admiral: If you had made that decision, you would not be here now."

"Where *would* I be? Washington?" He was caught up in the possibilities for a moment. "Running a corporate think tank on the Beltway?"

The hesitance was back. "This has not been a scenario it has been necessary to investigate before, so my estimates are perhaps faulty, but—"

"But what? Stop beating around the bush, dammit!"

A sound resembling air being forced through a bellows approximated a deep breath for the computer. "If you make that decision in 1990, Admiral, instead of the decision that brought you to work on the Project, there is an eighty-seven-percent chance that the time line will split. The 'you' that is in the year 1990 will continue on to work in Washington, but the 'you' who is in our own time will . . . just . . . disappear."

CHAPTER
EIGHT

The mall didn't close until ten on weekdays, and the after-dinner crowd was strolling and shopping, dragging the little kids along to look in the windows, hauling packages around. Teenagers in jeans and T-shirts and backward baseball caps clustered in the record stores, under the eyes of wary clerks. Exercise walkers puffed along the perimeter, arms swinging, leaning forward as if momentum would keep them going when energy failed.

Stenno and Lisa cruised through an anchor department store, looking over the rack of junk necklaces and cheap earrings. Stenno was wearing headphones, dancing in a jerky, arrhythmic fashion to the almost-audible music as he examined a pendant, let the chain slide through his fingers as he spun away, picked up several cards of earrings and tossed them in the air, juggling, caught them all and tossed them onto a nearby counter. The saleswoman from the perfume counter across the aisle observed him nervously and picked up a house phone to mutter a few words.

Lisa, watching her from the end of the jewelry counter, turned into the display of fine scarves. As three store security people converged on Stenno, she slipped a Hermès silk into her purse and calmly worked her way out of the area.

Stenno had nothing on him except the radio, a gold credit card, and a driver's license, both of the latter indisputably his. He was perfectly willing to turn out his pockets for the security people, and even apologized for making the perfume counter saleslady nervous. He'd been looking for a gift for his girlfriend and gotten distracted by the song; he'd be happy to take himself (and his gold credit card) somewhere else. . . . By the time he was through, all four store personnel were apologizing to him, and the saleslady was offering him a selection of free samples.

Lisa, waiting for him at the fried-pie stand, giggled at the tale and kept touching her purse, peeking inside at the heavy gold-and-green silk. Finally Stenno slapped her hand away.

"What are you trying to do, tell the world you've got something in there? Don't you have any brains at all?"

She was shocked silent a moment, her eyes wide. "I . . . I, I'm sorry—"

"Hey, baby, it's okay." Stenno leaned forward, kissed a crumb of pastry from the corner of her lip. "You did real good. You did just like I said, and it worked just like I said, didn't it?"

"Yes," she whispered.

"And it'll work the next time. You've just got to learn to stay cool, even afterward. You don't act like some kind of kid with something special in your purse! People will want to know what it is.

"And it isn't that special. It's just a damn scarf." His hand touched her throat. "It's real pretty, baby, but it's not as pretty as you are. It's not as special as you are. You think that's special, baby, you haven't seen special yet. . . ." He kissed her again, lingeringly, and a pair of six-year-olds behind them made disgusted noises.

Lisa flinched, glancing around self-consciously, but Stenno pulled her closer. "What's the matter?" he murmured into her hair. "How come you care so much about what other people think? You ought to care what *I* think, baby, not anybody else. *I'm* the one who loves you, right? Right?"

"Right," she responded, arching herself toward him and casting a defiant glare at the children. "Right. You love me, even if nobody else does."

Stenno, deeply involved in nuzzling her neck, grunted affirmation.

Jenniver Wales was burrowing into her embroidery basket, looking for the scissors, when the pain struck again. Her husband looked up at the hiss of air sucked between clenched teeth.

"Did you say something, dear?" His attention was still focused on the TV, where a commentator on the public television station was deep in talking-heads discussion with a representative of state government. It could have been mistaken for a hard-hitting hour of "Meet the Press" if the representative in question had only left his Stetson at home.

"Oh, nothing. Just got a little stitch in my side." But her husband had already forgotten his inquiry, and she eased herself back in the chair and closed her eyes, preparing to wait it out. This was the second attack this evening—the second in less than three hours. She hoped that it was just a fluke. If it happened too often Stephen might notice.

Standing in the doorway to the living room, Sam paused at her words and wished that Al was around. He wanted to know what was wrong, and what he could do to help; but Jenniver had made it clear that his interference was less than welcome. . . . He could see the white line on her lower lip where the woman was biting down, distracting herself from the pain she couldn't control with a pain she could.

Across the room, oblivious, Wales sprawled back in his recliner-rocker, dead pipe clenched in his teeth, and gave full, furrowed-brow concentration to the problem of grazing fees for government-owned land. The clock on the mantel chimed nine-thirty, barely audible above the conversation on TV and the wet rasp of breath through pipestem.

"The faucet's fixed," Sam announced.

The professor acknowledged him with a wave of the hand, never taking his eyes from the screen. His wife's expression opened sufficiently to send him a tight little smile. Sam started to say something, anything, to bring Wales's attention to the woman's pain, but the pleading in her look forestalled him. And the attack was passing, he could tell; she was beginning to straighten up, take deep breaths again. If he said anything now, she would simply deny everything.

Frustrated, he left the house and returned to the apartment over the garage.

It was unfortunate that Ross Malachy's tastes in fiction were so close to Sam's own. Most of the books Malachy had, Sam had already read; he could close his eyes and call most of them back to memory without effort. His textbooks were neither challenging nor interesting. Sam toyed with the idea of writing a paper for his inadvertent host, in part payment or apology for the loan of the kid's body. But that would be cheating, and besides, a paper on "The Psychological Impact of Repeated Temporal Displacement: A Study in Time Travel" would never get past the professor, much less into the hands of the peer reviewers.

Still, the idea had some appeal. He could write up some notes of his own; when he got back home (he quashed without mercy the stab of longing the thought gave him: *home*) he could do a paper of his own.

But there would be no peers available to review his work, either. Nobody to examine the validity of his data. And it certainly wouldn't be a reproducible experiment. He shuddered. He wouldn't wish a ride like this one to be reproduced by his own worst enemy, scientific method or no.

He spared a moment to wonder if he had a worst enemy, and if so, who it might be, or why.

"You're your own worst enemy," a voice in his memory said. *"You care too much about people. When are you going to learn that they're never going to care about you as much as you care about them?"*

"They don't have to," he answered. The sound of his own voice in the empty room startled him, and he looked around to find the speaker and ended up laughing at himself.

It would be nice, though, to be able to fill in that particular hole in his memory. Who had tried to convince him that he cared too much?

But it was gone. He had long since learned not to agonize over the holes in his memory, at least the less-than-life-threatening holes. It was still annoying when they shifted around, and he could remember being able to remember something that he couldn't remember anymore, but agonizing over it buttered no parsnips, as his mother used to say. As best he recalled, anyway.

But the kid had some nice music, and a CD player—surprising extravagance for a poor student? Maybe not. Sam found some Broadway cast originals and put them on, settled cross-legged on the floor and reached for a stack of papers, looking for still more clues about his current host. Usually Al would tell him what he needed to know, but if Al was staying away, he needed all the mundane help he could get.

Ross wasn't into physics, and had just enough French and German to squeak through a language-competency exam for graduate school. But he was sharp on sociology—only nineteen, freshman age, and already taking graduate classes. He had a background in statistics, "a background" being a nice way of saying he knew somebody who was good at it. Judging from some of his papers, stacked in a box underneath the desk, he was a little shaky on some of the more advanced concepts.

"Don't ever go to Vegas, Ross," he murmured.

"Why not? I like Vegas."

It was difficult to spin around from a cross-legged position, particularly when one has adapted a half-lotus position. Sam ended up half on his back.

"I always told you that stuff wasn't good for you," Al said, cocking a bushy eyebrow at the tangled legs before him. "Yoga. Dumb."

"I didn't hear the Door," Sam said. "I thought you said you weren't—"

"We oiled the handlink. And I changed my mind. A guy is entitled to change his mind, isn't he?"

Sam allowed himself a classic double take, knowing that Al would take the meaning of the look. The hologram nodded in sharp agreement. *He* knew when he made a role-reversal comment; he didn't need Sam Beckett's droll expression to tell him.

Before checking out of the Vegas hotel, he had changed from the purple-and-pink into one of his favorite, bright red faux-leather suits with the matching fedora. It didn't occur to him that the droll expression could have been occasioned by the outfit.

The CD changer clicked and began playing the score to *The Music Man*. Sam thought about trouble, which starts-with-T-and-that-rhymes-with-B-and-that-stands-for-Beckett, and took a deep breath. "Well, I'm glad to see you."

"Thought you would be." They traded quick looks. Al, never good at the mushy stuff, broke first, busied himself with the handlink, poking at the cubes that controlled the multimedia input. "Well, we got some stuff, but—"

"But what?" Sam scrambled to his feet and tried to circle around Al to see over his shoulder. Al pivoted to keep facing him.

"Well, it's awkward!"

"What do you mean, 'awkward'? And which one of us is leading?"

Al pulled his head back and peered up at the other man, confused. Sam indicated the handlink, his pointing finger passing through it. "I'm trying to read the thing."

"I don't know why," Al responded, "the screen isn't big enough for one person to read, let alone two. Anyway.

"I've been trying to get the information you need, but the problem is that you're too close."

"You said that before."

"I mean it this time." The words were out before he could stop them, and he had the grace to look a bit guilty as he went on, "There's been too much history lately. You had all that stuff built into the virtual encyclopedia when you started the Project, but it was just about that time that things started going nuts in Eastern Europe, and then the Common Market, and we never did get caught up. We've been loading the stuff from New Mexico from 1990 on, but most of the newspapers and stuff have to do with what the cuts in military spending are going to do to the Labs. There just isn't a whole lot on the Wales family, or the folks in his encounter group."

The glare warned Sam not to inquire, however innocently, about the one member of the encounter group that Al could be expected to have good data on. After all, Sam reasoned, there couldn't have been any changes in what Al did. He dismissed the thought. Al's breath of relief escaped him entirely.

"What about school records for Lisa? Medical records for Jenniver Wales?"

"Medical records? Is she sick?"

"There's something wrong. I don't know what it is, and I don't think she's told her husband about it. But I've caught her a couple of times looking like she was in a lot of pain."

"So maybe that's it, huh? You should tell Wales to send his wife to the doctor, and everything will be hunky-dory and you can get out of here?"

"You know Wales—knew Wales—better than I do. What do *you* think he'd say if his hired help told him his wife was sick?"

"Hmmmpfh. I see what you mean. He wouldn't like it much. Getting into his territory, and stuff."

Sam raised an eyebrow at this evidence that Al had, after all, been paying some attention to Wales's ideas. Al, ignoring him, poked at the handlink.

The voice of Robert Preston swelled over them both, obscuring the sound of a car door being slammed in the driveway below.

"Nope. Nothing yet." Al spoke to the blinking collection of Jujubes in his hand. "Gushie, see about getting that, willya?" His mouth twisted as he explained to Sam, "The records aren't in any kind of civilized database, and they're tough to even scan. We may have to *keyboard* it."

"*Quel horreur,*" Sam remarked.

"If you're going to be snide, at least be snide in a civilized language," Al muttered. Sam merely grinned.

The sound of a doorbell being rung repeatedly split the pause between tracks on the CD. The ringing was followed by the flat sound of a palm against a door, and a yelling, "Mom! Dad! Open up!"

"Oh, no," Sam murmured, moving over to the window. Al came up beside him, his holographic image moving partway through both the daybed and the other man in his effort to see what was going on. A light by the front door, triggered by a motion detector, illuminated the yard and the figure of a young girl alternately punching at a doorbell, pounding on the door with her fist, and attempting to peer into the living room through the drawn curtains.

"That's the kid?" Al murmured, keeping his voice down even though there was no need to do so.

"Yeah." Sam's voice was quiet too. Quiet, and filled with the beginnings of anger. At whom, he wasn't quite sure yet; the girl was making enough racket to raise the proverbial dead. "I don't know what's taking them so long. It isn't like they can't hear her."

Lisa continued to call, her voice becoming more and more raw as her parents did not answer.

The lights inside the house went out. Lisa fell silent.

The door remained closed.

CHAPTER

NINE

The two men waited, and the young girl waited, and all three realized at the same time that no one was going to open the door.

"Hey," Al protested to the unmoving door. "Let the kid in. It's dark out there. C'mon."

Lisa's shoulders slumped, and she looked somehow smaller in the harsh light. The leather bag slid down to the concrete porch.

She raised her head suddenly, as if she had heard a sound from within the house, but still no one came.

"They didn't really lock her out, did they?" Al muttered, chewing ferociously on his cigar. "That stinks."

"Looks like it," Sam said grimly.

The small figure at the front door bent down and picked up her purse.

"Now what's she going to do?" Sam asked.

Never one to take a question rhetorically, Al answered him. "She's gonna go find her boyfriend.

What'd they do, tell her if she went out she could stay out?"

"Yeah. I didn't believe them. I guess neither did she."

"So is this boyfriend really bad news, or what?"

Sam paused, remembering the snatches of conversation he had heard through the bathroom window. "Maybe."

"Well, if they lock her out for going out with the guy, what are they going to do if she spends the night with him? That's the thing that drives me nuts about parents. They keep making ultimatums way too early. No strategic planning— Hey, where are you going?"

Sam was already out the door of the apartment and halfway down the steps.

"Lisa!"

The girl, halfway down the driveway, turned to look back at the man calling her from the stairs. "Ross?"

"Lisa, where are you going?"

"Where do you *think* she's going?" Al said disgustedly, from the still-open door. "I told you—"

"They locked me out." Lisa's voice wavered between bewildered hurt and adolescent defiance. "If they don't want me, I don't have to stay, do I?"

"Where are you going?" By this time Sam had reached her, was looking down at her.

Lisa barely came up to Ross Malachy's shoulder. To meet his—Sam's—eyes, she'd have to tilt back her head. Make a positive effort.

She wasn't interested in making the effort. Sam found himself looking down at brown hair gleaming in the light from the corner street lamp, at thin shoulders shaking in the coolness of an evening breeze.

"Lisa?" He reached out, lifted her chin.

She was inhaling deep sharp breaths, one after the other, keeping her eyes squeezed shut, lips compressed, trying very hard not to cry.

"Oh nuts. I hate it when they cry. I can never figure out what to say." Al was in the middle of things, as usual, but this was a thing for which he wanted to fade to the perimeter.

Sam wasn't sure either. He could say, "Don't cry," but if Lisa didn't want to admit that she was teetering on the thin edge of lost self-control, it wouldn't be tactful to tell her that her efforts were wasted. On the other hand, if she wanted comfort—

She wanted comfort. With a wail, she threw herself into Sam's arms.

"Ah, now this is different. I could always figure out this part." Sam's glare shot daggers at the hologram, who raised his eyebrows and shrugged. "Well, it worked for me."

Sam bit back a scathing reply and patted the sobbing girl on the back. "Lisa, please—"

"They hate me! They *want* me to go away!" Lisa pulled away, dashing tears from her face, and went on with a dazzling lack of logic, "Well, if that's what they want, that's what they'll get. I'll be the dutiful daughter, all right. I'll go away and I'll never come back!"

Somehow the words made her look even smaller, more fragile in the uneven light. Her handbag swung from a clenched fist. She was wearing artfully torn jeans with an abbreviated lace top, and makeup so heavy it might have been from the sixties. Al circled her, looking her up and down.

"Jailbait," he concluded.

"Jailbait?" Sam repeated, startled.

"Jailbait?" Lisa echoed, equally startled. "Are you calling me jailbait?" she continued, outraged.

"Yep," Al said.

"*No!*" Sam almost shouted, equally frustrated at Al and Lisa both.

Lisa stepped back, through Al, with the force of Sam's response. "That's what you said," she pointed out. She might be backing away, but she wasn't backing down. Al looked down at the blur that was himself transposed onto a teenage girl and hastily moved away.

"You are not jailbait," Sam said, biting off each word. "You're just in a little bit of a mess right now, and you don't have anyplace to go—"

"Yes I do," she interrupted.

"Sure she does," Al reminded him helpfully. "She can always go to—"

"Stenno's."

Both men blinked at the facility with which the girl completed Al's sentence. Al nodded decisively. "See? Told you so."

Lisa was still standing, watching Sam, as if waiting for him to comment. Cars coming down the street caught the two of them, Sam and Lisa, in their headlights, pinning them to their shadows in the driveway. Al, who had no shadow because he was the man who wasn't there, was neither illuminated nor pinned.

"Lisa, don't go to Stenno's." It sounded lame, even to Sam.

"Give me one good reason why not."

"He's—Lisa, your parents care about you. They don't want to see you get into trouble. They don't want to see you get hurt."

"So they lock me out of the house? I don't see them being worried about what happens to me. At least with Stenno I'll have a place to sleep."

"And somebody to sleep with," Al added, an unnecessary parenthesis. Sam glared again. Al smirked back at him with a Welcome-to-the-real-world, Sam-Beckett look. "Hey, I didn't say I thought it was right," he pointed out.

Sam shifted his attention back to the girl. "Lisa, how old are you? Fifteen? If you go to Stenno, you could both end up in a lot of trouble. You're underage."

"Not in New Mexico, she isn't. Fourteen is statutory—no, wait, I think they changed that law. About time, too." Al was busy poking at the handlink. "Ziggy says the age of consent for females is now sixteen in this state. Still too damn young if you ask me," he added as an editorial aside. Sam wondered in passing if the hologram was trying to interpret the data from the handlink by the light from the street lamp or from the Imaging Chamber, dismissed it as irrelevant.

"But at least Stenno *wants* me." Her lips were beginning to tremble again. "And I don't have any-place else to go."

"You can stay in my apartment."

"I *knew* you were going to say that," Al groaned. "Sam, that is a *really* dumb idea. Her father's going to have a fit if he thinks—"

"Where are you going to be?" The quavering had been swallowed, and she was staring at him speculatively, a little unsure about what Sam was saying.

"Good question," Al observed. "If she stays with you, Daddy's going to really blow his top. You're going to get Ross thrown out in the street, and it isn't going to help her one bit."

"I can always find someplace to go," Sam assured her, ignoring Al. "Come on. You go upstairs. I'll, I'll go stay with friends or something. We can sort things out in the morning."

"You don't have to go away," Lisa said.

"Uh-oh." Al winced. "You're in trouble, Sam. This little girl thinks she's not so little."

Lisa came closer to Sam, her lithe figure swaying. Her mascara was smeared in streaks down her face. The shadows cast by the leaves dappled both of them. "I wouldn't want to put you out of your place. You could stay. It might be fun." She smiled, ran a hand over his chest. Sam caught it and held it still. The wind lifted her hair, tossed it lightly across her face, and she ducked her head gracefully to get the errant strands out of the way. She looked considerably older than fifteen years old.

"Yeah, if you were about three years older," Al observed. "Sam, you know better than to fall for this."

Simultaneously, Sam said, "Lisa, you know better than that. You're in enough trouble with your father. Don't make it worse."

"*I* should have known better," Al muttered. "Mr. Resist Temptation At Any Price. Sheesh."

"My father hates me. He doesn't care what happens to me. He locked me out!" The facade of seduction crumpled, and the girl looked younger than her age instead of older, scrubbing at her face as the tears started up again. "I don't have anyplace—"

"I'll talk to your father," Sam tried to reassure her.

"It won't do any good. He won't listen. He never listens. You saw him. He hates me because I'm not a boy."

"That's not true, Lisa. He's your father, he loves you. He just doesn't know how to say it very well."

"Got any more platitudes to trot out?" Al said, as Lisa began crying again. "The ones you've got don't seem to be working."

"I'll talk to him." All three participants, physical and hologram, jumped as a new voice joined the conversation.

Lisa stepped hastily away from Sam as from the shadows at the side of the house, Jenniver Wales, dressed in a frayed house robe washed out by the night lights, stepped forward. "I'll tell him I opened the door for you. Come on in to bed, Lisa, it's late. You need to get your rest."

For one long moment Sam thought Lisa would defy her mother too. Then, shrugging, the girl twirled her purse over her shoulder and passed her mother, going around to the side of the house.

Jenniver paused in the act of turning to follow her daughter. "Thank you, Ross," she said with dignity. Then she wrapped her arms around herself and went back into the house, leaving man and hologram staring after her.

"Lordy, lordy," Al sighed. "That could have been real interesting, Sam."

"Yeah." Sam swallowed, more shaken than he had any intention of ever letting Al know. He might be in his forties, might tell himself he was older and wiser and well in control, but Ross Malachy was only nineteen, and had all the right hormones for dealing with a teenage girl on a late spring evening.

"Maybe this is what you have to fix," Al said. "Straightening out Lisa. If it is, you've got your work cut out for you."

"I don't think that's it," Sam said, shaking off a paralysis of staring. "I don't think you can straighten out a teenager in one Leap. It takes more than that."

Al thought about that, nodded agreement. "Yeah. Takes at least eight years, and you still don't get to a conclusion. But this has got to be part of it."

Sam led the way back up the steps to the apartment. "Did you know about the problems Wales was having with his daughter?" he asked, holding the door open for his friend as if he were really there.

Al flinched. "No. Look, just don't get me involved in this, okay? Pretend I'm not really here really. I'm not going to make any difference at all, right? So don't pull me into it."

"Hey, okay, okay. Don't get so upset. I only asked for some information." Sam, brows knitted, watched him walk through a cabinet. Generally Al tried to observe the "reality" he shared with Sam, going around the objects which were solid in Sam's moment even though they were only holograms to Al, just as Al was only a hologram to Sam. Al tended to forget to observe the proprieties when upset or worried or distracted.

"Yeah, right." Al tugged on the rim of his fedora and made a show of examining the handlink.

All three, Sam decided. Upset, obviously, by Sam's Leap into a reality that included a version of himself; worried at the possibilities inherent in the situation; distracted by the whole subject.

"I just thought you might remember something that Ziggy didn't have in the database," he said cautiously. "You know. Available resources."

Al stopped pacing. "Hey, it was years ago for me. A lot of water has gone under the bridge since then, if you know what I mean. I'm not going to remember trivia about some kid and what trouble she got into with her dumb boyfriend." He shook his head, resumed pacing, and tossed over his shoulder, "And what do you mean, 'available resources'?"

Sam laughed, trying to break the tension that vibrated in the little apartment. " 'It makes sense to use all the available resources.' That was one of your favorite sayings. God, you said that so many times. Remember? Back when I was designing Ziggy?"

The look Al gave him sent chills up Sam's spine. It was confused and wide-eyed and totally blank. After a long pause he said, "Uh, sure. Yeah. Of course I remember that!"

"That was what gave me the idea for the combined neurocell technology," Sam went on, a sick feeling growing in the pit of his stomach. "I can remember that. That day you agreed to join me. That was the most important day of the whole Project, we both agreed. I didn't want to do it, take the cell sample, but you said it again, about a hundred times. You talked me into it. 'You have to use all of your available resources,' you said."

Al was staring at him, growing steadily paler.

97

"You remember, don't you, Al?" Sam could hear himself pleading.

"Of course I remember," the hologram whispered. "How could I forget anything that important?" He swallowed convulsively. "Uh. Hey. I think I hear Tina calling me." Stabbing at the handlink with an index finger, he summoned the Door to the Imaging Chamber, and with one last stricken glance he disappeared through it. Sam watched as the Door slid shut, leaving him alone.

More alone, perhaps, than he had ever been in a Leap. He was almost used to the idea that his memory was less than reliable, and that for reasons he didn't quite understand, Al would never tell him everything about the Project that he wanted to know.

But this was the first time that he had remembered a conversation so clearly, only to find that Al had no idea what he was talking about. As if the conversation he remembered had never happened at all.

CHAPTER
TEN

Two hundred feet under the earth, beneath the cin-
derblock houses that were the superficial appear-
ance of the Project, beneath the Accelerator and the
Imaging Chamber and the Waiting Room and the
Control Room, down in the cold chambers, lay the design offices, the guts of the computer irreverently
named Ziggy. One corridor was lined with cubicles,
with desks and drawing boards and small computers,
some linked and some not. Once the cubicles had
been occupied by members of Ziggy's design team,
each handling a separate set of challenges in the
building of a new and unique computer. The design
work was done. As a result, most of the little offices
had been abandoned for several years.

At the end of the corridor were two larger offices,
one belonging to Tina, one belonging to Sam. Al
turned the knob on the door—the Project Director
merited an office with a door—and went in.

99

Al had asked Sam once why he needed two offices, one down here and one up on the Control Room level, and Sam had shrugged and waved his hands incomprehensibly. It made sense to him, and that was enough. In the upper office he took care of administrative things. Down here, he had worked on Ziggy itself. More than worked on: he had created the computer. Once it was up and running, he had returned here sometimes for further study, for consultation with his creation, or for a really challenging game of solitaire, as far as Al knew.

There was no one at all on this level at this late hour except Al, and the computer which was always present. He could hear his footsteps, and tried to walk more quietly. He looked in each of the cubicles as he passed. The air was filtered and chilly; there was no dust on the desks or screens to reveal how long they had been abandoned. Except for the lack of loose paper on the desks, everyone might have left for lunch, planning to return in an hour with noise and life and movement. But it wasn't true, hadn't been true for a long time.

There were no books in Sam's office. Scanners, yes, lots of scanners. A huge video screen, and a hologram table in front of it to play three-dimensional images upon. Against one wall, a lab table, with an old-fashioned microscope; biological isolation chambers and instruments that Al never did understand. There was even a glove box containing a Petri dish filled with something that looked like yellow wax.

In this room, in a rite ridiculously like pledging blood brotherhood, Sam had taken nerve cells from Al's hand. He needed them, he'd said, because he couldn't create the neurocells for Ziggy using his own substance alone. Ziggy would be the product of the two of them. Al assumed that Sam had used nerve cells from his hand too, but he was never sure just when he first noticed the lock of white hair at Sam's left temple. He had long since decided that he had no Need to Know.

It was a concept that Al tried very hard to forget. No one knew where the cells came from but Sam and himself—and the computer. It was easy for the computer to link the two of them so Al could be the Observer; man and machine and man were all an unbreakable chain. As soon as Ziggy could pin down when Sam was, it could always home Al upon him. No one else could be the Observer. It drove Tina, who was responsible for the physical construct of everything except the neurocells, absolutely out of her mind. She refused to design with the new cells. Sam had done all of that.

As Al stood, looking around the office and trying both to remember and not to remember, the giant screen came to life.

"Admiral." The voice was a woman's. Sometimes Al missed the deeper voice Ziggy used to have, once upon a time. He and Sam still referred to the computer by the masculine pronoun, even though it sounded more like an alto since Tina had made her adjustments.

The greeting was an acknowledgment of his presence, and considerably more polite than the computer was accustomed to being. The screen had gone from blankness to an ever-shifting fractal pattern, interrupted from time to time by a cartoon character tromping his way wearily across the visual field.

"Hi, Ziggy." Al settled in Sam's chair, twirled around looking for a place to put his feet up.

There was no place but the desk itself, and the chair teetered alarmingly as he tried.

"If you pull out the lower right-hand drawer, you'll be able to prop yourself on its edge." The screen chuckled in blue and green.

"I thought Sam kept those drawers locked."

"Not in this office," the computer advised him.

"Oh." Al hauled the drawer open, flipped through it inquisitively.

"Anything interesting?" the computer said dryly.

Al jolted back; he would be blushing if he remembered how. "No. Nothing." He settled back, put his feet up, and rolled his unlit cigar between fingers and thumb.

"Was there a particular reason you decided to visit this office, Admiral?"

Al didn't answer for a moment.

"Admiral?"

"I heard you." He stuck the cigar between his teeth and laced his fingers across his belly.

"Well?"

"You're awfully impatient for a computer," Al said. Long practice allowed him to talk around the cigar without spitting.

"We measure time differently, Admiral." The images on the screen began blinking, changing, one per second, steady as a clock.

"All right, all right. What do we have?"

"I fail to understand why you are deliberately delaying accumulating the necessary data to—"

"Stow it, Ziggy. I'm ready to hear it. Now."

"Yes, sir." The screen blanked. "The latest data has not yet been scanned into my data banks, but Gushie did obtain the local newspapers covering the

102

relevant period, from 1990 to the present."

"And?"

"Data pertaining to the Wales family is remarkably sparse. However, we have determined that Dr. Wales continues to teach his support group for several years."

"Okay. So what?"

"Mrs. Wales dies approximately eighteen months from Dr. Beckett's present, from ovarian cancer."

"Ouch. That could be it—"

- "And Lisa Wales is currently in prison, serving a ten-to-life sentence for second-degree murder."

Al dropped his feet and his cigar, simultaneously. "Second-degree murder? That little girl?"

"The crime for which she was convicted occurred in 1997." The screen blacked out for a few seconds, then came back up again, blood red.

"What happened?"

"Lisa Wales was tried and convicted in 1990 of murder of a shop owner, in the course of an attempted robbery. However, she was a juvenile, and her records were sealed—"

"So how did you get hold of them?" Al asked, momentarily distracted.

"I have my methods," the computer said with dignity. "Her records were sealed. When she was released, she showed no signs of rehabilitation and in fact shortly developed a serious drug problem. The arrest for the 1997 murder was her third— not counting the juvenile crime." As the computer spoke, an image appeared on the hologram pad, showing video footage of a Lisa Wales who looked thirty years older than the fifteen-year-old that Al remembered. Her hair was long and stringy, there were dark circles under her eyes, and her face was gaunt and pale. Her hands were shackled together and chained to her waist. The clip showed her stumbling and mouthing an obscenity to a sheriff's deputy escorting her down a featureless hallway.

The clip ended, ran again. Al shook his head. "That must be it, then. Sam's got to stop her from doing that first one. What else do you know about this juvenile crime of Lisa's? She killed somebody while robbing a store?"

"I am still attempting to access the details," Ziggy admitted. "I am not certain. There is an eighty-five-percent chance that Lisa did not commit the actual murder in this case. However, as an accessory, she would be considered just as guilty."

"And Dr. Wales just keeps teaching. Whew. At least one member of the family stays normal."

"As you say." The computer sounded doubtful. "I will continue to investigate. Meanwhile, I suggest that you give Dr. Beckett the details as soon as possible. The probability is extremely high that the reason for this Leap is to prevent Lisa from participating in the robbery."

"When exactly does it happen?"

"I have been unable to determine that. I project that it will occur sometime within the next seventy-two hours, however."

"Okay." Al stood, pushing the chair back, and then paused. "Oh. Something else I meant to ask you."

"Yes?" Ziggy sounded impatient. Sam had programmed a number of human characteristics into his creation, among them a more-than-healthy ego. It was, Al considered, one of the biggest mistakes the genius scientist had ever made, right up there with stepping into the Accelerator in the first place.

"Have you ever heard me use the phrase 'You have to use all of your available resources'?"

"No," the computer replied promptly.

"You're sure I never used that phrase?"

"Not in the past leading to the current moment," Ziggy qualified. "You may have used it in some other past."

Al sank back down in the chair. "Always before, we knew when the past changed. When the senator changed, for instance, I knew both pasts. Hell, I had to—I was sitting there watching!"

"The other members of the Senate subcommittee did not seem to realize there had been any change," Ziggy pointed out pedantically. "For them, the history with Senator Diane MacBride was the way history had always been."

Al waved his hand, dismissing the observation. "They weren't linked in to Leaping. My point is, when Sam changes something, one or the other of us knows it. But now neither one of us remembers me saying that, and Sam claims I used to say it all the time."

The computer hummed to itself, the graphics on the screen jerking slightly.

"It would seem," Ziggy said slowly, "that Dr. Beckett is remembering a past which neither of us can recall."

"I just said that."

"If that is indeed the case," the computer went on, ignoring Al's interruption, "it may be that Dr. Beckett's course through time is diverging so radically from the past which led to my creation that . . . the fact of my creation may be threatened."

105

Al swallowed. "If you disappear, Ziggy, what happens to Sam? Will he never have Leaped?"

"I don't know." The graphics program froze, blinked out of existence. "I will have to consider this problem."

"Well, don't consider it so hard you skip getting into those court records of Lisa's—"

"I may not be able to control the amount of resources I devote to it," the computer said. The feminine voice was almost whispering. "I've never wondered before—"

The voice stopped, and Al waited for it to go on. Finally he broke the silence. "What? What haven't you wondered? I thought you thought about everything."

"But I never thought about death before," the computer said. "Death is for you mortals. But if Dr. Beckett doesn't create me, am I really here?"

CHAPTER
ELEVEN

It was Saturday morning. Sam awoke to the trilling of birds in the cottonwoods, tense and alert.

It took a few minutes to remember where and when and who he was this time. Once reviewed, he lay there and listened, eyes closed. It wasn't often that he was able to just—rest.

In the distance he could hear the hum of traffic, probably on Central—even early on a summer Saturday morning there would be traffic. But Central Avenue, part of the old Route 66 of song and story, was almost a mile south of the Wales house, and the neighborhood was strictly residential. Unlike the newer parts of Albuquerque, in this neighborhood old-growth cottonwood trees growing on either side of the road met in places. They shaded the asphalt from the heat and insulated homes in the area from turmoil and unpleasantness. The little apartment over the garage was peaceful and quiet.

He'd have to get up and do things soon. Once upon a time he used to jump up as soon as he was awake, ready to face the world and a thousand tigers, but lately, the opportunity to just lie still, eyes closed, and feel the rhythm of heart and lungs without stress, without terror, without the need to leap up and save others from themselves or from the monster of the week was. . . just . . . wonderful.

Butnofarmboycouldremainabedfortoolongwithout feelingguilty.Theremightnotbecowstomilk,butthere weredragonstoslay,somewhere.Reluctantly,Samrose, showered, and dressed.

Unfortunately farm boys also got used to big breakfasts. A multi-degreed genius might have tempered his yearning for cholesterol in all its many forms, but Ross Malachy was still a growing boy. And there was absolutely nothing in the apartment to eat.

Ransacking the refrigerator yielded a six-pack of soda. There was nothing else. Disgusted, he checked his wallet. There wasn't much there, but if he remembered right, the Frontier Restaurant, a campus hangout across the street from the university, had terrific breakfast burritos and cinnamon rolls. His mouth watered at the thought.

"Ross! Mom says are you gonna come eat breakfast or what?"

It was Lisa, of course, whose idea of summoning began and ended with standing at the front door and yelling at the top of her lungs. Sam sighed and opened the door.

"Coming!"

Breakfast was nothing like dinner of the night before. Dr. Wales was already finished with huevos rancheros and the sports section, leaving the folded-back pages exposing headlines that read "Denver Can't Lure Thompson" and "Chiles Hope to Recover from Recent Lack of Kick." Sam, seeing the latter out of the corner of his eye, did a double take; it wasn't a misplaced food-section story after all, just a column about the local soccer team.

Jenniver Wales bustled about, smiling like June Cleaver in jeans, preparing another skilletful of eggs and chile; tortillas were already standing by. Lisa was eating dry toast and orange juice and keeping a low profile. Sam was relieved to see that Wales didn't seem inclined to take official note of the previous night's argument. With a grateful smile he put the first forkful into his mouth, chewed, and lunged for a glass of milk.

"Does okay with the chile, does she?" Al said from behind him. Milk escaped up Sam's nose, and he grabbed a paper napkin. He had forgotten what homemade huevos could be like. His eyes were tearing, his nose was running milk, and he was trying valiantly to swallow the mouthful without completely disgracing himself.

"Need the Heimlich maneuver?" Al inquired mercilessly. "You always were a wimp when it came to good chile."

"*That* is *really* good chile," Sam gasped, clearing sinuses and mouth at once. Al circled the table. This time he was wearing one of his favorites, the red suit with the purple-and-red shirt and a bolo tie. He peered over Wales's shoulder, reading the sports scores, and nodded. "Crummy team," he muttered.

Sam didn't bother to ask which team was crummy. Al bet on them all, and one of them was bound to lose.

Jenniver, meanwhile, was nodding at the compliment. "Makes up for all those blisters in the fall," she said. "Would you like some more?"

"Blisters?"

"Roasting chile." Al poked at and drew circles in the air with his cigar, emphasizing. "You always get blisters roasting chile, it comes with the territory. Then you freeze it and you have vitamin C all year round." Lisa walked through him on her way out the door.

"Oh, I was just joking." Jenniver held up the spoon interrogatively. Sam nodded and continued eating a little more cautiously, with frequent sips of milk to coat his mouth, esophagus, and stomach. It was good, but his mother would have had conniption fits at the thought of spicing eggs that way.

"Well," said the professor, putting the newspaper aside, "I'm going to get some work done on that paper. Remember what I told you last night about getting ready for our group, Ross. It's disruptive, not having everything in place when you need it."

"Oh. Sure." Sam swallowed the last mouthful. "I'll take care of it."

He folded his napkin and picked up his plate and silverware, carrying them over to the sink and winning a grateful smile from Jenniver in the process. "Why, thank you, Ross, that's very thoughtful of you."

He shrugged lightly, glanced over his shoulder. Stephen Wales was gone. He took a deep breath.

"Um, Mrs. Wales, I couldn't help but notice last evening you seemed to be in some pain—"

Her smile vanished. "Don't be silly, Ross."

"I saw," he said. The woman clearly didn't want to discuss the matter, but Sam had a stubborn streak.

"Ziggy says she's going to die in a few months," Al said. "But that isn't the important thing—"

"It is important," Sam said, interrupting the hologram and startling Jenniver with his intensity. "You were in pain," he went on, addressing the woman now. "It could be really serious. Have you seen a doctor?"

Jenniver Wales, standing against the kitchen counter, had stiffened and withdrawn, leaning backward to create more distance between herself and "Ross Malachy." Sam stepped back to reduce the pressure on her. It was a mistake.

"Ross, I have to tell you that this is none of your concern," she said firmly. Her face was pale, and her right hand moved up to push back hair that was still in place. "I appreciate your concern, but I'll thank you to mind your own business."

"Ross's" jaw dropped. "What?" he sputtered.

"Mind your own business, Ross." With that, she turned around and turned on the faucet, determinedly clattering the dishes together. The message was clear: The conversation was at an end.

"Sam, will you listen to me for a change?" Al complained. "There's more going on than this."

"But she's going to die," Sam murmured.

Jenniver froze for a moment. Then she hunched her shoulders and slammed a pot lid down, sending a spray of soapy water across the counter.

"Sam, will you please get somewhere I can talk to you?" Al snapped, exasperation in every word.

"Okay. Okay, fine." Sam withdrew to the otherwise-empty living room, Al floating along after, clutching the handlink as if at a lifeline. Which in a sense, of course, it was.

Ensuring they were alone, Sam spun on Al. "What do you mean, she's going to die but it's not important? How can it not be important? If she gets to a doctor in time it could save her life!"

"According to Ziggy, it's already too late."

"Ziggy isn't always right!"

"There's more going on than this," Al insisted.

"How can you say a woman's life isn't important!"

"Okay, okay." Al raised his hands in surrender. "Maybe 'not important' wasn't the best way to put it—"

"It sure as hell isn't!"

"All right, it isn't!" Al was getting rather red-faced himself. "I'm sorry. Is that what you want?"

"Words are cheap," Sam muttered, still angry.

Al chose to ignore the comment. "You can't do anything about Jenniver, but you *might* be able to do something about Lisa." The shorter man stood his hologrammatic ground while Sam paced, ending up staring into the fireplace, one hand supporting him as he leaned against the mantelpiece.

"What about Lisa?"

Al outlined the history that the computer had discovered. By the time he was finished, Sam was facing him once again, giving him his full attention.

"What store? When? And where's her father in all this?"

"We don't know yet," Al confessed. "The records were sealed, so we know more about the later murder. The one she's in prison for now."

"That doesn't help me. If I can prevent her from getting involved in the first one—"

"Ziggy says the chances are nearly one hundred percent that she won't—wouldn't?—*won't* be in prison today. She's on a slippery slope, and she's too close to the edge for comfort."

"But the kid is going to lose her mother, too."

"Ziggy says there's no way you can prevent that."

Sam shot him an agonized look. "I don't believe that. I can't believe I've Leaped in here to find this out and can't do anything about it."

"You can't solve everything," Al pointed out.

"I never said I could. But whatever makes me Leap always puts me in a situation that needs to be fixed, a situation I *can* fix!"

"That's true," Al said. "But I'm telling you, Sam, Jenniver Wales is not that situation. You're here to keep Lisa from screwing up her life."

"Can't I do both?" Sam whispered.

"I don't think so, Sam." It hurt Al to see his friend torn up that way, but there was nothing to be done. Jenniver Wales had ovarian cancer, and in the very best of cases her chances of survival would have been poor. In this case, the cancer was far too advanced. Jenniver Wales had eighteen months of surgery, chemotherapy, and radiation treatments to look forward to, complicated by seeing her only daughter arrested, convicted, and sent to jail for murder. From Al's point of view, her death would be nothing but a merciful release.

He could understand Sam's feelings, though. One of his friend's degrees was an M.D., and even though Sam's Swiss-cheese memory didn't allow him to remember his medical skills—or even, always, that he had a medical doctorate—nothing could change his need to help, to try to relieve pain. It was a delicate kind of torture to stand by and do nothing, either because the person whose body he was occupying couldn't possibly have the kind of knowledge Sam Beckett had or because Sam Beckett couldn't remember what he himself knew.

"Ross? Are you looking for something in here?" It was Stephen Wales. "I thought you were going to be down at the hotel, setting up." The professor looked significantly at his watch. "Three o'clock this afternoon, you know."

"Time for the tom-toms," Al muttered.

"You would know," Sam muttered back, out of the corner of his mouth. Stephen Wales looked startled.

"I'll take care of it right away," Sam said hastily. He started to back out of the room, then paused. "Ah, Dr. Wales—"

"Yes?"

"I realize it's none of my business, but I've noticed that—"

"Ross, are you still here? Good. I need some more dishwashing liquid. Please pick some up for me on your way out." Jenniver Wales stalked forward, holding out a five-dollar bill. As Sam reached out to take it, she added, "I need it right away. Please go now." In a much lower tone, inaudible to her husband, she added, "I told you that my health is none of your business. If you want to keep this job, you'll remember that." There was nothing faded or uncertain about her look.

Al nodded sharply in agreement.

Sam sighed.

"Yes, ma'am."

"What do we know about Ross Malachy?" Sam asked suddenly. Al, who had somehow arranged to be seated exactly as if he were in a truck, complete with elbow resting on the window ledge, glanced over in surprise.

"Ross? I don't know. I forgot to ask about him."

"You *forgot to ask*?" Sam was incredulous. "You've got the guy sitting there in the Waiting Room and you forgot to check into *his* future? What if the person Lisa kills in this store robbery is *me*? Did you ever consider that possibility?"

Al looked startled. "To tell the truth, no. We've had other things on our minds."

"Like what?"

Al cleared his throat and pulled his arm in, started fiddling with the handlink.

"You know, I wish you'd cut that out. Half the time I think you're just doing that to have something to do with your hands." Out of the corner of his eye, Sam could see the furrow of exasperation in Ross Malachy's forehead, reflected in the side mirror. He shook his head and drummed his fingers on the steering wheel, realized that the drumming was just as much a nervous habit as the handlink-fiddling he'd just accused Al of, and stopped himself, wrapping his fingers around the wheel at ten and two o'clock, exactly as the driving manuals recommended.

Al was giving him a guilty look as he continued surreptitiously poking at the little machine.

"So what's been so important?" Sam said.

Al cleared his throat. "Well, you know. Problems with computer chips, data download, stuff. All the usual stuff."

"I must not have done a very good job designing that computer," Sam muttered sourly.

The handlink squawked indignantly.

"Oh no, no, you did a great job. A fantastic job. But, you know, it's a maintenance problem."

"Yeah, maintenance. That's the ticket." Sam didn't believe him.

Al gnawed his lip. "So," he said, in a transparent effort to get the subject back on track, "what're you going to do about Lisa?"

Sam, watching the traffic, shrugged. "I don't know yet. I've got to stop her somehow."

"Ziggy said the robbery happens within the next seventy-two hours. No—the next forty-eight hours, now. He's reviewing the data now." Al poked surreptitiously at the handlink, sneaking glances at Sam as if he expected to be caught at it.

"With all the newspapers in this town, you'd think he would have it figured out by now." Ross Malachy had musician's fingers, long and narrow, and Sam caught himself drumming them again.

"You know, you get awfully damned cranky sometimes!"

Sam remained silent as he changed lanes, got on the I-40 on ramp, merged with eastbound traffic, headed toward the blue-and-purple mass of the Sandia Mountains. Al waited him out, as stubborn as his friend.

"Okay. Okay, I'm sorry," Sam said at last. "I just get tired of living my life according to Ziggy's percentages sometimes. Ziggy says that he figures Lisa's going to get in trouble, but he doesn't have any details yet; but I know for sure that her mother's sick, and you're telling me that I can't make any difference. I want to make a difference, Al. I'm here to make a difference. Otherwise, there's no reason for any of it, is there?"

Stenno Baczek knew better than to stride through the mall wearing a black leather jacket and dark glasses, his shoulders rolling to make them look bigger, his elbows out to hit the window shoppers as he swaggered. There was a time and a place for everything, and this might be the place, but it sure wasn't the time.

When you were cruising the mall, showing colors or just having a good time, it was okay to scare the civilians. It was fun to play chicken with the security guards, not quite crossing the line where they'd have to hassle you and yet making it clear that you were better than they were, man, you were so free, and they—they wore uniforms.

But when you were planning to work a place, then you wanted to fade in while you checked places out. Just act like a regular kid. Look at stuff, buy some stuff, see how they handled the merchandise, how they handled the cash. See how they reacted to teenagers. See who was vulnerable.

Besides, it was too damn hot to wear black leather today. The weather report on the radio this morning had said that the city was going to have a record high, that the temperature would hit 101 degrees today. So you wore a T-shirt and cutoffs and acted like the rest of the crowd. It wasn't all that difficult.

You could even buy some soft pretzels and lemonade and sit on one of the benches so conveniently scattered around and watch the flow of people while you delicately picked the salt crystals off and crushed them between your teeth, savoring the bitter taste. The pretzel would be warm and chewy and soothing; the lemonade sharp and cold and sweet.

Some stores were wrong to begin with. Music stores, for instance. Way too many people in the music stores. You could never get in and out in time, not in a music store in a mall. They were always packed, right up to quitting time.

Jewelry stores were bad too. While he yearned for the delicate gold chains in the window, the clear stones that caught the light and tossed it back like laughter, jewelry stores were too well protected. They had alarms and the mall always stationed somebody nearby. Only a fool would go for one of those, and Stenno never considered himself a fool.

Same with drugstores. Last year a friend of his had tried to hit a drugstore. Rick didn't know that the pharmacist taught a gun safety course in his spare time; he'd made his haul and he was on his way out the door when some old lady got in his way, and the next thing he knew he was on the floor coughing up his own blood. That wasn't how Stenno envisioned himself, either.

But there was that notions shop. Stenno hid a grin behind another sip of lemonade. The customers were mostly women; they wouldn't give him any trouble. The store never had a big crowd of customers at any one time, but it did a surprising amount of business, mostly in cash. He watched as the proprietor, a slender Asian woman, bustled around, straightening up a display of buttons. There weren't any customers at all in there now, even though the mall was in the middle of the midmorning rush. And he'd had his eye on the place for a while. Last night she'd even pulled the wire barrier down almost all the way while there were still customers in the store in her hurry to close up. She'd had to pull it up again to shoo them out, finally.

Of course, if he were to walk into a shop like that, all those females would take one look at him and they'd know he wasn't there to buy thread and rickrack. But that was okay. He'd have a girlfriend to drag him along. And once they were inside, well— he could look uncomfortable and self-conscious with the best of them, until it was time to empty that register.

Then he could pull the barrier shut behind the two of them as they left and nobody would even know.

He could even hang a "Closed Due to Owner's Illness" sign on the barrier so they wouldn't notice when she didn't open up the next morning. He chuckled to himself, earning a quick glance from a grandmother sitting on the bench across from him, rocking a stroller with her foot. He shook his head at her. *Just a funny thought, grandma. Ha-ha.*

He was wearing his trustworthy face, and she looked away, cooing at the sleeping baby. Stenno thought about what he'd do if she was in the store too.

No, he decided regretfully. She was one of those baby-sitting grandparents. She'd probably be missed.

Still, he could picture her sprawled out on the floor, crying probably. The thought made him chuckle again, and he unfolded himself from the bench and walked past her, glancing down at the baby as he went. She kept an eye on him as he paused to study the child.

"Cute kid," he said.

"Thanks," she said warily.

Stenno grinned, deposited his paper cup and napkin in the trash bin, and walked away.

CHAPTER

TWELVE

There are more PhDs per capita in the state of New Mexico than any other state in the United States.

New Mexico also has one of the lowest per-capita income rates in the United States.

Stephen Wales, PhD, sat at his study desk and thought mournfully about this.

Wales's doctorate was not in statistics.

Nonetheless, they were a depressing pair of facts. Wales certainly belonged to the first group; he suspected that he contributed to the second as well. If it hadn't been for the late addition of a couple of men to the latest group, he would have had to cancel the contract with the hotel. As it was, he'd just squeak by.

He rubbed at his mouth and looked at the figures again. Maybe it wasn't worth it after all. Maybe he *should* look into getting a job in some personnel department somewhere, administering personality tests to shifty employees. He was so tired of being grateful for Jenniver's biweekly paychecks. Teaching one class a semester at the university as an adjunct professor just wasn't enough, and they were always those damned introductory classes, too, with three hundred bored freshmen and the same old out-of-date textbooks. And this summer he'd barely managed to hang on to a mailbox in the psych department, much less an office.

But he wanted to *help,* dammit. He wanted to help other men find what he'd found, that it was possible to be male and emotionally healthy, to connect with other human beings as something other than an image, a stereotype.

Every time the drums sounded, he got closer to the essential truth of being a whole man. Strong, secure. Happy. At peace with his place in the world.

Stephen Wales needed the drums.

"Steve, honey, we need to talk about Lisa." It was Jenniver, a tired, determined look on her face.

He looked up, really seeing his wife for the first time that morning, shocked at the lines around her eyes and mouth. She was standing in the doorway, one hand holding on to the lintel. There was a water stain on the front of her clothing from washing the dishes. She glanced at the stack of bills and then back at him.

She was looking at him expectantly, waiting for him to shift gears to address what they were going to do about Lisa.

And he didn't have a clue.

Grasping at straws, he responded, "Can't you see I'm busy, Jen? Besides, she was at breakfast. There isn't any problem."

Jenniver wrung the dish towel around her hands, twisting it. "Yes there is, Stephen. We need to talk about it."

"Now that's where you're wrong, Jenniver. I've told you and told you, you can't impute your needs to other people. *You* may very well need to talk about it, dear, but I don't." He got up, took her by the shoulders, guided her out the door.

Real men didn't have to feel guilty about making decisions.

Al Calavicci's divorce lawyer amounted to an old family friend by now, even if Al had never stayed married long enough to start a family. Al hung up the phone feeling like he'd been talked to by the proverbial Dutch uncle.

He never left a marriage with much. He never wanted to be stingy, and besides, he didn't need much. He'd learned just how little he really needed a long time ago. Give him a good cigar and a chance to go to a ball game and he was happy. He couldn't seem to convince Dirk, his lawyer, of that; the word "skinned" came up in conversations frequently, but he could walk away from anything, whistling. There was always someone new around the corner.

For instance, that was a nice offer there, sitting on the table. Join a think tank. One of the Beltway Bandits. Of course, he couldn't advise on anything he'd been working on, but that wasn't a problem; he'd been so involved with the Star Bright Project that he never did get into other programs. But these guys wanted to speculate about the future of the Soviet navy, and he could speculate with the best of them.

Okay, so maybe all they wanted was to add an Admiral, USN (Ret.) to their letterhead. But they'd have to let him play with their toys *sometime*. And it was better than anything else on the horizon.

And with another alimony payment looming, he needed something. Good ol' Dirk knew that. He'd been hinting around about what Al's future plans were, but of course he wasn't going to come right out and ask.

It was great to be able to tell him that yes, there was a job out there. Al knew too many retired military officers who got tossed out into the real world with superb skills in military life, and no clue how to live as a civilian; too old to get hired, and even if they did, too far behind their "peers" to compete in the climb up the corporate ladder.

Things were definitely looking up.

So why didn't he feel happier about it?

He looked at his watch. In a few hours he could go down to the hotel banquet room and see about that group meeting. Dirk said that he needed to go, so Dirk could tell the judge that Al was still trying to solve his communication problems. Al snorted. Communication problems? *He* never had any trouble communicating. You couldn't say that a guy who'd been married five times had trouble getting his point across.

Other people had understanding problems, that was the truth of it.

Jenniver Wales paused by the telephone, her hand resting lightly on the receiver. She could pick it up.

She could call a doctor.

She could make an appointment.

She could take the car, keep the appointment.

She could tell the doctor about the pain. He could order tests.

But then there would be the bill. One more to add to the pile on Steve's desk.

They couldn't pay for it.

Maybe the pain was nothing, after all. It didn't hurt right now, after all.

And there was the dusting to do.

Her hand fell away from the phone.

Sam hated having to deal with hotel conference staff. The situation required courtesy and endless patience, smiling references to contracts he'd never seen, oblique references to nonperformance and damage-penalty clauses. This wasn't the kind of stuff he was good at. His father had raised him to believe that a man's word was his bond, that a handshake was as binding as any contract could ever be, and he'd absorbed those principles into his bones.

The perky little Indian girl, therefore, was enough to make a saint weep.

There was nothing derogatory about calling her "little." She was five feet tall if she stretched to her utmost. And "perky" was the precise word. He had barely entered her office when she was coming around her desk, hand outstretched, saying "*Hi* there!" in the most cheerful voice imaginable.

But would she ensure after-meeting coffee? Oh, she was so very sorry! she said, rattling her squash blossoms. She looked like a walking advertisement for an entire tribe of jewelry-makers who specialized in the garish. She had bracelets on each arm, silver and bearclaw and huge chunks of blue stone. She wore heishi and silver necklaces, with a red coral naja, a horseshoe-shaped pendant, that hung nearly to her concho belt. Her fingers were loaded with rings. The simplest, a sandcast with a malachite center, she wore on her left thumb. There wasn't room for it anywhere else. Sam had never in his life seen so much Southwestern jewelry on one person, not even in Santa Fe.

But there would be no after-meeting coffee. Nor was the hotel responsible for the safety of Dr. Wales's equipment. Sam caught a flicker of—something—in her voice.

"I guess you must think this whole thing is pretty silly," he said.

"Heavens no, of course not, Mr. Malachy! Dr. Wales is a valued customer!" Her hair was black, picking up red highlights in the reflection of the sunlight from the hotel pool outside her floor-to-ceiling office window. She had a wonderful view. Looking over the top of the rooms on the other side of the glittering waters of the pool, he could even pick out the tiny black sticks that were the transmission towers on Sandia Crest, the top of the ten-thousand-foot mountain looming on the eastern border of the city.

Of course, anybody in the pool had a wonderful view of her, too. Sam thought that would drive him crazy, not being able to work in privacy. But maybe this woman was used to it. She certainly seemed to be—she never glanced once at the people staring in.

"Well, if he's all that valued, it seems to me that you could do a little extra for him. At least make sure that what he needs is there when he needs it. I don't think that's too much to ask."

She pouted disappointment. "Oh, I really, really wish we could, Mr. Malachy! But that's what contracts do, you see. When you've signed them yourself you'll understand better, I'm sure."

She was seeing Ross Malachy, age nineteen, and she was talking down to Ross Malachy. But it was Sam Beckett who responded. "I'm sure that when Dr. Wales signed the contract, he expected that reasonable efforts would be taken by the hotel to provide security from the time we bring things in until the meeting actually starts. At least lock the room! It's not as if we're talking about all day, Ms. Clearwater."

"So no one will steal your 'ceremonial drums'?" she said. "They must be very precious to the doctor."

There it was again, that flicker of something. But this time she'd been a little too obvious. Enlightenment dawned at last.

"It's the drums that bother you, don't they?" Sam said. "You don't like the group and you don't like them using drums."

"It *is* a little disruptive to the rest of the guests when they get so loud," she said with a moue of distaste.

"You think they're doing an imitation powwow, don't you? Making fun of Indian dances."

The temperature of the room dropped noticeably. "Mr. Malachy, that sounds a lot like a racist remark."

"You think Dr. Wales is ridiculing something that should be important."

Suddenly the perky veneer vanished, and she leaned across the table, dark eyes snapping. "Don't tell me what I *think,* Mr. Malachy. Don't assume you know everything about me from my looks, and don't condescend to me. I've worked in the conference business for fifteen years, and in this hotel for the last three, and I've never had a group like yours before. Sitting around with your shirts off, talking about getting in touch with your emotions—

"But what a bunch of foolish men choose to do with their spare time has nothing to do with me. Dr. Wales has a contract for the use of that room. That's all he has a contract for."

"You're absolutely right," Sam agreed. "It doesn't matter, as long as what goes on is legal. And it's legal."

Her rings clicked together as she drummed her long nails against the desk pad. "What's your point?" she said at last.

"My point is that we need a service from this hotel that any reasonable person would agree is more than fair. It won't hurt you in the least to provide it, and it would be good customer service."

"On one condition," she said.

"What?"

"Dr. Wales has to put a sign up on the doors to that room that says what's going on in there. I can't begin to tell you, Mr. Malachy, how tired I am of people coming to me asking when the dances were going to begin, and if it would be okay if they took pictures, and what tribes we had in there. And then they start asking *me* questions as if I were a walking advertisement for the Gathering of Nations!" She looked down at her hands, the rings on the fingers clenched tightly together, and smiled wryly. "Well, maybe I can understand that part. But it would make my life a whole lot easier if he just put up a sign."

"Sure, we can put up a sign." Sam sat back, slightly bewildered. "Is that all? We could have done that ages ago. All you had to do was say something earlier."

"It wasn't in the contract," she pointed out.

"Neither is coffee," he responded. "Besides, you can always give people who ask questions about dances directions to the Intertribal Cultural Center. That way you'll be making *all* your customers happy."

She grinned.

He left the hotel feeling pretty good about himself. It was a silly, trivial dispute made that much worse by leaping to unwarranted conclusions.

Leaping. Sam chuckled to himself. He'd been guilty of that a few times. In fact, you could even say that Leaping to conclusions was what his life was all about these days.

Which reminded him of the conclusions in this situation. The chuckle ceased abruptly. The Waleses were due for such incredible misery if he didn't find a way to change things—but he couldn't seem to find the key.

Al was convinced that it was Lisa, and Sam had to admit, reluctantly, that something did indeed have to be done. He just wasn't sure what. It'd be nice if Ziggy could come up with something more concrete about the robbery and how it went down.

"Went down"? He'd been watching too much television. Or listening to Al too long. Sometimes it amounted to the same thing.

Pulling into the driveway of the Wales house, he saw Lisa going around the corner, heading for the back yard.

He looked at his watch. It was nearly noon.

He got out of the car and followed her.

129

The back yard was thick with lilies and Bermuda grass. One giant cottonwood tree shaded a patch of ground into empty pale brown dirt. Lisa was sitting on the edge of the patio, next to the barbecue grill, her arms around her pulled-up knees.

She glanced sideways at him as he stood beside her. "Is this space taken?"

She shook her head, silently. He folded himself down to sit beside her, plucked up a strand of Bermuda and began tearing the green leaflets off, one by one.

"Things are pretty rough, huh?" he said, not looking at her. Across the yard, a pink climbing rose was beginning to flower against the cinder block wall. Underneath the rosebush, a stray robin was investigating, looking for worms in the pale brown soil. That rosebush was going to need sand, and feeding, he thought absently. Roses didn't do well in earth that was practically pure caliche.

"They're okay," Lisa mumbled. Her bare toes, already tanned from exposure to the sun, twisted in the creeper-strands. Her cheek was pressed against her knee. She was wrapped up into a tight ball, her toes the only venture into the summer heat.

"Y'know, I used to fight with my folks sometimes." He had, too, but never like the fight last night. He couldn't imagine his sister Katie yelling at his mother the way Lisa yelled at hers, or his father locking him out of the farmhouse where he'd grown up. He wondered briefly if Ross Malachy had ever fought with his parents that way.

A ladybug crawled over Lisa's big toe, paused, lifted its black-spotted wing covers and flew away. She scrubbed the place where the insect had been with the toes of her other foot. "It tickles," she explained.

"Yeah. Look, Lisa, your parents really do love you. Look at what your mom did last night. And your dad couldn't have meant it—he didn't even say anything this morning."

She shook her head, turning it away from him, but not before he'd caught the betraying stripes of tear tracks sliding past her nose.

"They're worried about you. They don't want you mixed up with the wrong people, making some terrible mistake."

"I'm not mixed up with the wrong people!" she sniffed defiantly. The sun glinted in her hair, and the ladybug, unnoticed, landed on her head like a tiny ornament. He raised his hand to brush it away, and then lowered it again, leaving the gemlike insect alone.

"But they haven't got any way of knowing that," he said reasonably. "They look at a guy like Stenno, and of course they're going to be worried. If you go off with him and don't tell them what you're doing, they imagine all kinds of awful stuff."

"I'm only fifteen. What kind of awful stuff could *I* do?" Her voice was young, immortal, and full of scorn.

"Oh, get off it."

She raised her head at the sudden absence of sympathy in his tone. "Whaddaya mean?"

" 'I'm only fifteen. What kind of awful stuff could *I* do?' " he mocked. "You know better than that. Kids your age could get pregnant, or get hooked on drugs, or get AIDS, or be part of a gang. Kids your age drive DWI and get killed."

"Dad won't let me get my license," Lisa said resentfully.

"Oh my— Lisa, are you even listening to me? Juvenile is filled with kids even younger than fifteen. There's a lot out there to be worried about! And your parents know it. They're responsible for you. They love you."

"Yeah, well if they love me so much, how come my dad locked me out? He knew I was out there. He even turned out the lights and went to bed."

Sam drew a deep breath. "He's not perfect. He makes mistakes too."

"So how come he gets to make mistakes and I can't make any?"

"He's trying to teach you that mistakes have to be paid for. He told you to do something and you disobeyed. He told you what the consequences were going to be, and he had to follow through." Sam had spotted the logical fallacy in this long ago; he only hoped that the girl hadn't.

Unfortunately, she was a smart girl.

"That's pretty dumb. I coulda gone away. I coulda stayed with *you*. What would that teach me?" She was sitting up now, rubbing her knees. There was an old scar on the right one, pale against the tan. "So Daddy locks me out, and Mom lets me in. Big deal."

"Okay, it was a dumb thing. He should have done something else, something that would stick. I guess he knew that. Maybe that's why he didn't say anything about it this morning. Maybe he was afraid to start another fight. You're not the easiest person in the world to get along with, you know."

That got him a narrow glance through the fringe of brown bangs.

"But that doesn't change the fact that they're your parents," he went on, "and they still have the right to know about Stenno, and where you go with him, and what you do."

"That's like saying *I* haven't got any rights! I can go where I want and have my own friends. They can't tell me what to do."

Sam was beginning to feel baffled and frustrated and immensely sympathetic to Stephen Wales. The feeling of triumph from his encounter with Ms. Clearwater at the hotel had disappeared entirely. "They're your *parents*, Lisa. They *love* you."

"They do not," she said decisively. "They just want to boss me around. I know who really cares about me."

"Who, Stenno?"

But there was just a touch too much sarcasm in his voice, and she rose to her feet in one lithe movement, standing over him and blocking out the sun.

"Yeah, Stenno cares about me. More than they do. *He* wouldn't lock me out in the middle of the night." She slapped her hands against her shorts and stalked off.

As she went, the ladybug flew away.

CHAPTER
THIRTEEN

The first man stuck his head in the door, looked around the empty room with an "I'm not sure I'm where I'm supposed to be" look on his face. Seeing no one else around, but with the familiar large drum up on the podium, he sidled in along the wall and stood uncertainly, a gym bag in his hand.

Five minutes later two more men came in, and the first man, seeing the door open to admit them, immediately unzipped the bag and stuck his hand inside as if he had just arrived himself.

By the time Sam arrived with Stephen Wales, the entire group had arrived. Including, Sam was amused to see, Al Calavicci, who was standing in the middle of a circle of men playing one-up games about hot dates. Calavicci caught the smile in his eye and waved him over.

"Yeah, kid, *you* ever dated a redhead?" somebody asked. "You know what they say about redheads. . . ."

"My sister's a redhead," Sam said with a straight face.

"Ooops," Al muttered, turning a bit scarlet about the ears.

Sam smothered a chuckle. He had no idea if Ross's sisters were redheads, blondes, brunettes, or bald. But he seemed to remember that one summer Katie Beckett had experimented with henna. The veggie-head summer, as he recalled it.

Wales was standing in front of the podium, calling the group to order. Al hung back with Sam as the rest of the men trailed over.

"Hey," he said, "I'm sorry, I didn't mean—"

"That's okay," Sam said cheerfully, "you never do. You'll learn one day." He walked off, leaving the shorter man staring after him, thoroughly confused.

Wales arranged the men in a rough circle. Gradually the muttering quieted down, and they stood attentively, their eyes on him. Al slipped in among them, standing beside Sam. Stephen Wales was standing a little taller.

"We are men," he intoned.

The men standing around him avoided glancing at each other.

"We are men," he repeated. "We are men who have been abandoned by the world we built. The world jokes about us, the world says it no longer needs us, the world legislates against us. But we are met here today to remind ourselves that we are still men."

The poor guy, Sam thought.

"We are wise. We are important. We are special."

The circle of men moved uneasily.

"We *are* special," Wales repeated. "Lyle Walker, tell me who you are."

The man standing three from Al's right jerked, startled. But he'd heard the question before, and he knew the expected answer.

"I'm a man," he said. "My name is Lyle, son of John. I'm a man."

"Tell me what you've done."

"I've . . . I've gone to school. I've held three good jobs. I've fathered four kids."

"How does this make you feel?"

"Proud. Happy." Lyle smiled suddenly, as if he had just realized that he really was proud and happy.

Wales smiled back at him, and went on. "Mike Diaz, tell me who you are."

"I'm a man," said a heavyset Hispanic to Sam's left. He, too, was familiar with this litany. "My name is Michael, son of Robert. I am a man."

"Tell me what you've done."

"I've built a summer cabin with my own hands. I've got two kids of my own and adopted four more, and they're all in school."

"Tell me what you feel about that."

"I do good work. My kids are good kids."

"How do you *feel*?" Wales insisted gently.

"I'm proud . . ." But Diaz seemed uncertain.

"And?" Wales prompted.

"Sometimes I'm scared. So much can happen these days. I get angry."

"Good!" Wales approved. "You have important feelings! This is very good!

"Jess Piciouski, tell me who you are."

"I'm a man," said a slender blond man across the circle from Sam and Al. He seemed uncertain. "Um, my name is Jess, and my father's name is Vincent, ah, Piciouski—"

"You are the son of Vincent," Stephen Wales prompted gently.

"The son of Vincent," Jess corrected himself, looking around to see if anyone was laughing. No one was.

"Tell me what you've done."

"I, I don't know." The man was fair skinned, and was turning a bright red.

A muffled, visceral groan went up from the circle.

"Hey *yaaa*," Mike Diaz said.

"Hey *yaaa*," Lyle Walker responded.

"Hey *yaaa*," other men chimed in.

"You're the sum of all the things you've done," Stephen Wales said to the blushing victim. The chanting softened, a counterpoint to his words. "How old are you, Jess?"

"Ah, twenty-seven," he stammered. The men beside him had put a hand on each of his shoulders, and the whole circle was swaying, a low-key, subtle sway, in time with the chant.

Sam found himself swaying with them, almost but not quite sharing the chant; beside him, Al swayed, too. You couldn't stand in a circle like this one and *not* sway with them. It was an oddly supportive action. Jess seemed to think so too; at least, his answers were getting more confident.

"Are you married, Jess?"

The blond man cleared his throat. "No."

"Do you have children?"

"No."

"Are these requirements to be a man?"

"No!" the circle chorused.

"Men think that being a man is about sex, about being different from women. This is true and not true. This is part of being a man, but being a man is more than that. Being a man is being a son, a brother, a father, an uncle, a friend. If a man has no family, he can still be a friend. But all those things are about what we are in relation to other people, and what we speak about here is what we are in relationship to ourselves.

"Being a man is about courage in adversity. Being a man is about honesty. Being a man is about trust. Being a man is about facing the things we fear, the things that make us uncomfortable, and being reliable anyway.

"Being a man is about knowing your pain, welcoming it as the friend who tells you that you are alive. It is right to cry, to know when to cry. It is right to feel pride in what you have done. It is right to laugh.

"Being a man is about acknowledging your soul."

The men glanced at each other. They were less uncomfortable now. They were all the same now. They had an experience in common. If they'd been doing this for a while, Sam thought, they had a lot of experience in common, closed in this room. They might not acknowledge each other if they were to meet in Sears Automotive, but here, inside this room, something else was going on. What happened here was not about paying the bills and answering to the boss on Monday morning; it was about feeling important, feeling part of a mysterious tradition, a long line of fathers and sons stretching back through history and into the future, of having an essential place.

"Al Calavicci, tell me who you are."

Sam shot a quick glance at Al, who was swaying and humming with the rest of them. Al was older than the rest of the men here, not noticeably, but at least by a few years. And for all his excitability and passion, he wasn't the kind of man to easily give away his feelings to strangers.

But he too was caught up in the sound of the drums. "I'm a man," he murmured. "My name is Al. My father's name is—was—Guido."

His sharp, dark eyes snapped open to meet Wales's, just as the other man was about to correct his phrasing as he had for Jess. Something in the look in Al's eyes silenced the correction, and Wales went on with the ritual questions. Al mumbled some response, evoking a halfhearted supportive "hey *yaaa*" from the men next to him. Sam, who had been holding his breath, let it go. He couldn't imagine Al talking about his relationship with his father, or about being an admiral, or being a POW. Not in a group like this. Al's realities were too harsh for this bunch. He'd found out the hard way, long since, what it was to be a man.

The questions went on, skipping over Sam, much to his relief. Perhaps Dr. Wales didn't want to embarrass him for his lack of life experience, he thought with grim amusement.

The meeting went on in the same general vein for another hour, with the rest of the participants each giving the name of his father and what he had done. When they were finished, they pulled out chairs from the gurneys and set them up in a circle. Wales told them a story about a prehistoric boy going on his first hunt, and suggested to them that they had each had the equivalent of a first hunt. He asked for volunteers to tell their own stories. Only three could come up with something: one man told about the first time he'd fixed his car by himself, another had ridden a bicycle across Canada's Northwest Territory, the third had enlisted in the military. Sam, by this time sitting cross-legged on the floor next to Al, could feel Al suppressing a snigger. Sam decided he was just as well pleased that Al chose to keep his own tales of his personal rites of passage to himself. He had heard them, from time to time; they were never quite the same from one telling to the next, but they always had certain elements in common. Perfume and prowess, mostly.

Wales brought the meeting to a close, and they got up, with varying degrees of stiffness, and went over to talk to each other and Wales, to get dressed again for the real world. Sam decided to put the podium and chairs back the way they had been originally, a gesture of thanks to Ms. Clearwater whether she ever heard about it or not.

"Hey, kid."

Sam looked up, startled, from stacking chairs onto the gurney. It was Al, the physical, here-and-now, drab version. Sam almost called him by name, but checked himself. Ross Malachy didn't know Al Calavicci by name, and wouldn't address him that way if he did. But he'd take the proffered right hand, once the ever-present cigar was switched to the left.

He made some uncertain responsive noise, and Al introduced himself.

"Ross Malachy," Sam responded. "Nice to meet you."

141

"You work for Wales, huh?"

"It helps with tuition and stuff." Sam went on folding down chairs.

Setting the cigar between his teeth and talking around it with the ease of long practice, Al remarked, "I thought all you students got by with grants and scholarships." He began folding down chairs too, and passing them over to Sam to put on the transport. In moments they had fallen into a working rhythm.

Sam laughed, remembering his own undergraduate days. "Even scholarships aren't always enough. Just living can be expensive."

"Tell me about it," Al agreed feelingly. "Got a family?"

"Nope, just me." The last few chairs were stacked and ready to go. "Hey, thanks for the help."

"No problem." Al was staring at him steadily, as if trying to see through him.

A sudden chill went through Sam. If the Al of the future could see Sam, no matter whose body he temporarily occupied, why couldn't the Al of this moment too? He wondered who or what the other man saw as he studied him. Was it the younger, dark-haired, blue-eyed Ross Malachy, whose black-Irish ancestors had marked him as theirs for anyone with the eyes to see? Or was it Sam Beckett, taller, older, brown of hair and eyes and identical to the man this Al Calavicci had worked with less than a year before on Project Star Bright? Or did he see both at once?

How much recognition was in Al's eyes?

"Is something wrong?"

"Huh? Oh, no, it's just that you really remind me of somebody, and I can't figure out who. Something about how you talk, or move, or something. Ever had that happen to you? Where somebody reminds you of somebody else?"

"Not in quite that way, no." Sam pushed the gurney of chairs over against the wall. He looked around to see Wales deep in discussion with three of the other group members.

"You just haven't lived long enough, kid. Sooner or later everybody reminds you of somebody else."

Sam hid a wry smile.

Al had turned away by this time. "Wonder what the hell these guys think they're getting out of all this," he muttered, mostly to himself, but loud enough for Sam to hear. Sam had the feeling he was meant to hear.

"Everybody comes for their own reasons, I guess." He tried valiantly to refrain from continuing, and lost. "Why do you come?"

"Because my divorce lawyer and my mediator says I hafta," Al growled.

"How come?"

"Because otherwise my wife's gonna skin me alive."

What, again? Sam nobly refrained from saying. He wasn't supposed to know the guy had been married before. He shouldn't be playing along with the conversation, either, but he didn't want to walk away and leave Al standing there by himself, either.

"How come?" he repeated.

"They think I can learn something from this guy Wales. My divorce mediator read some article he wrote and said I had to come. I made the mistake of saying I thought all this stuff was horse puckey, and of course my wife was all for it."

"So you don't figure you're getting anything out of this?"

"Course not." The cigar was in Al's hand again, describing curves and tangents in the air. "This how-to-be-a-man stuff—*I* knew how to be a man when I was only—"

"I don't think that's what Dr. Wales means," Sam interrupted. Some things about Al would never change, and his one-track mind was one of them.

Al shot him a narrow glance. "God, you remind me of somebody. I just can't put my finger on it. . . . Anyway, it's all a crock."

"I don't think so. I think he's talking about recognizing what you've accomplished. Giving yourself credit. A lot of people never learn how to do that." He shrugged. "Feeling good about yourself means you need to have things you've done to feel good about. A lot of these guys don't realize just how much they've done with their lives."

"Not my problem," Al growled. "I know all about my life, thanks."

"You're luckier than most." *Luckier than me, that's for sure,* Sam added mentally. "Who's your divorce mediator?" he went on, casually.

"Oh, you wouldn't know her. She's in Washington, D.C. Where my wife is."

Sam affected puzzlement. "Then how come you're in Albuquerque?"

"Business with the Labs." Al didn't seem disposed to elaborate. Sam, who had an idea what kind of business was involved with the national laboratory based in the central New Mexico city, didn't ask him to. Most of Sandia Laboratories' budget was devoted to weapons engineering for the Department of Energy, and Al was in the military. Conclusions weren't hard to leap to.

"Anyway my wife told her I was coming here, and they cooked up this idea between them that I should attend this thing of Wales's while I was here. Made it part of the mediation package."

"So is your wife doing a women's encounter group session back in Washington?"

"Oh, sure. Every day. She calls it 'lunch.'"

Sam couldn't help it; he laughed. After a moment Al laughed with him. Sam moved off to put the drum in the truck, and Al went on his way.

CHAPTER

FOURTEEN

Sam had just finished locking the back end of the Blazer and was turning back to the sidewalk when Stenno hit him, a solid punch under the ribs that doubled him up. Only the bumper of the vehicle kept him from sliding to the asphalt in an inelegant puddle of amazement.

"Lisa says you've been hitting on her," Stenno said. His voice was casual, almost as if he were remarking on the remarkably hot weather they were having.

Sam was too busy gagging to acknowledge the remark.

"You stay away from her, or you're going to get worse than that. You understand?" Now there was a definite threat in Stenno's voice, and a thread of anticipatory pleasure too.

Sam could see the point of a boot pulling back, out of his line of vision, presumably to return at a much higher velocity. He shook his head, put one hand down on the bumper and tried to lever himself back on his feet.

"Hey, what's the problem here?" He recognized Al's voice, but it seemed to come in stereo, from behind him and in front of him at the same time. Lurching upright, he looked around.

Yes. There in front of him was Al, going nose to nose with Stenno like a terrier with a German shepherd. The kid was looking down at the older man with a mixture of contempt and disbelief. The two of them were so close together they could smell each other's sweat.

And *there* was Al, now standing to his left, his expression just as concentrated. Sam straightened up, carefully, looked from one Al to the other. The hologrammatic Al was ten years older, a little grayer, his clothing a lot more colorful; he was wearing a long-sleeved red shirt and an open black/red/gold vest. His trousers matched the shirt. He was scowling, gesturing with the cigar, holding his fists as if ready to punch Stenno if the kid made another move.

Whereas the "real" Al, drab by comparison in a short-sleeved dark blue cotton polo shirt and khaki slacks twin to those he had worn the day before, merely stood his ground, balancing on the balls of his feet. His hands were hanging loose, not balled into fists; somehow that was more threatening. Some snippet of memory blinked into being for Sam: a sensei demonstrating the posture of readiness, the ability to move in any direction, meet any threat without offering any threat of his own. Al had that. But as far as he knew, Al had never had any martial arts training. . . .

148

Stenno had no such snapshot of remembrance to draw upon, but he knew when he was too close to his opponent to use his longer arms and greater stature effectively. He stepped backward. Both Als followed. Stenno stepped back again and almost lost his balance over the concrete parking bumper. The "real" Al put out one hand, caught a flailing arm before the boy fell over backward, and pulled him back up again. Once he had done so, he immediately backed off.

"Got to be careful about those things," he said.

Stenno opened his mouth and closed it again. Sam, now back on his feet and rubbing his belly ruefully, could tell he wanted to pick up where he'd left off. But it was difficult to maintain a threat once you'd looked foolish. He shot a warning glare at Sam anyway as he turned to go.

"You okay?" Al asked.

"Yeah, sure, I'm fine." He could see the hologram Al mimicking his answer, with an *oh, sure he is* look on his face. "I am, really," he said again.

The real Al looked as skeptical as the projected one. "If you say so. I'd keep an eye out for that kid if I were you. He looks like he has a personal problem."

"In more ways than one," Sam agreed.

"You're sure you're okay?"

"Oh yeah. Sure I'm sure. Really!" he snapped, as the projected Al sneered. "But thanks for your help," he added belatedly to the real Al. "He kind of took me by surprise."

"Yeah, I'd say so. You be careful."

"Yeah, he could come back for more," the projected Al added, and winced immediately, as if he had said more than he meant to say.

149

"I can take care of myself," Sam said.

The real Al raised his hands in surrender. "Okay, okay. A word to the wise, that's all. Hate to see you kids fighting." He got into a white sedan a few cars down from the truck and pulled out, gesturing a cigar-laden wave as he passed, but without looking back.

"Thanks," Sam added to the remaining avatar. "Really."

"You're welcome," Al replied, staring off after himself. "Boy, this is weird."

"You can say that again." A couple of hotel visitors were staring at him as he talked to apparently empty air, and he fished out his keys and got into the truck.

"What about the doc?" Al said, floating into the back seat, where he wouldn't have to try to duplicate the seating conditions of the truck for the sake of Sam's visual equilibrium.

"He's having dinner here with a couple of the guys from the group," Sam said. "I'm supposed to come by and pick him up later if he doesn't call first and tell us he's got a ride home."

"Hmmmmph." Al added the data to the handlink and studied the pattern of blinking lights.

"What did you mean back there?" Sam asked as he pulled into traffic.

"Back where?" Al had a suspiciously innocent look on his face.

"When you said he might come back. You were there. *Did* he? *Does* he, I mean?"

"Hey, don't look at me, it was ten years ago for me!" When Sam said nothing, Al heaved a sigh. "Look, Sam, I *don't* know. Ziggy doesn't know. Things are all screwed up. Hell, you could have turned that guy into a pretzel if you wanted. You didn't need me back there. But how was I supposed to know ten years ago that the kid I kept from getting stomped in a parking lot was really my buddy who *at the very same time* was a couple hundred miles away putting together a Project I didn't have any part of?"

"I don't know about the pretzel part," Sam said. "I sure didn't see him coming, and he hits pretty hard for a kid." His hand crept reflexively across his stomach. "Do you mean you don't remember?"

"I don't know if what I remember is what really happened." There. It was out.

"I thought you remembered everything. I thought Ziggy had everything in memory."

Al shook his head. "Not this time, Sam. You're too close to yourself."

"That doesn't make sense," Sam argued. "The whole theory says I can only go back within my own lifetime. Why should 1990 be any worse than 1957 or 1973? I was alive then too."

"But in 1957 and in 1973 you weren't in the process of building Ziggy."

"So what if I Leaped to, say, 1998?"

Al grew thoughtful. "You started to Leap in 1991 . . . so you'd be double-Leaping. There wouldn't be a . . . no, that isn't right. . . ." He looked up, indignant. "Hey, you're supposed to be the genius, not me. Seems to me that if you Leaped into somebody in 1998 when you were Leaping at the same time into somebody else, your—your soul, or whatever it is—would be in two places at once."

"Well, isn't it now?" Sam didn't look at Al as he asked.

"No, of course not—what is this, me trying to explain your own theory to you?"

"Somebody has to." There was a suppressed bitterness in Sam's voice.

Al chose to ignore it. "When you Leap now, it's the same you, okay? One piece of string. The 'you' that's digging the tunnels for the Project is you, all right; he's you before you started Leaping. It's like folding that piece of string back and forth on itself.

"But if you Leap into a time after you started Leaping, you might really be in two places at the same *time*. And that would screw everything up."

Sam shook his head, skated through a yellow light, dodged around a bicycle rider in the middle of the street. "I dunno. Doesn't sound right."

"Well, the only way you're going to figure it out is if you get your memory back, and I can't help you with that."

"Because of those rules you say I made up."

"Yeah."

"Well, what if I just un-made them?"

Al looked uneasy. "Could we not talk about this?"

Sam beat his head against the steering wheel.

"I found out about Ross Malachy," Al said hastily.

"Yeah, so?"

"He's working as a research assistant for a multimedia encyclopedia company. Married, two kids."

"So?"

"So there's nothing to change about his life. Ross Malachy has a perfectly ordinary boring life, and never showed any sign that he was ever cut out for anything exciting. Ziggy says you Leaped into him because he's just plain ordinary. He's the only stable thing about the whole setup. He isn't the one who gets killed. In the original history, he wasn't even around when the robbery happened."

"And *when* did the robbery happen?" Sam said through gritted teeth, as he pulled into the driveway of the Wales house.

"Sunday—tomorrow night—at the mall. The notions shop."

"Ziggy got any suggestions about how I'm supposed to stop it?"

Al shook his head.

CHAPTER

FIFTEEN

Lisa stood in front of the gun cabinet, jiggling at the lock and frowning. Stenno wanted one of her father's guns. He didn't say why. She wanted to ask, but he got that look on his face and twisted his hand in her hair and pulled her head back, not yanking, no, he never yanked, but pulling. Just hard enough so she knew.

He told her to open the cabinet, but he never said what to do if the cabinet was locked.

She didn't think that he'd accept the excuse.

He wanted the gun tonight.

A gun, on Saturday night?

She fingered the little padlock hanging in the hasp of the cabinet, concentrating on the padlock, thinking only about the padlock. She'd already tried twisting it, and it wouldn't break. There had to be a key somewhere, a small key. Her father probably kept it with him all the time.

But if he didn't, where would it be?

Glancing around the room, she paused at the sight of the walnut desk. If the key to the cabinet was anywhere, it would be in the desk where he spent all his time writing and stuff. She dropped the lock and went over to investigate.

The drawers to the desk caught sometimes, and she had to get underneath to release the drop lock. As she climbed out again she almost bumped her nose on Ross Malachy's blue-jeaned legs.

"Lose something?" he asked blandly.

"None of your business," she said, getting to her feet without any offer of help from him. "What are you doing in here anyway? My dad's going to be mad if he catches you looking at his papers." Backing against the desk, she reached behind her with her fingertips and tugged at the drawer in the middle. It slid out easily. She didn't think Ross saw; he was looking up at the other side of the desk. She risked a quick glance over her shoulder; it wouldn't do her any good if her mother walked in. But there was no one there. They were alone.

"That's a funny kind of desk," he observed, standing in her way so she couldn't get past him. "It has one of those long rods that go through the back of the drawers."

"So what?" As long as the middle drawer was open just a little, the latch couldn't catch again. She could come back later and look for the cabinet key.

"Sometimes the lever holding the rod gets stuck and locks all the drawers, and you have to go underneath and release it so you can open things up."

"Will you please move?"

But the direct approach wasn't working. He was still looking down at her. Ross had the bluest eyes she'd ever seen, and she'd had a secret crush on him for a long time, right up until she met Stenno. He was tall—well, he was taller than she was, anyway—and lanky, and he had that gorgeous soft curly black hair. She used to dream that he'd stand close to her like this, look deep into her eyes this way, and say something really romantic.

Not, "What are you trying to get out of your father's desk, Lisa?"

"Nothing!"

Ross looked up again, past her. It was creepy, as if he was listening to something or someone. He shook his head sharply, started to say something, looked at her and changed his mind. It was spooky. "Don't lie to me," he said.

"If you don't move," she said with sudden inspiration, "I'll scream."

A look of pure disgust crossed Ross's face. He was about to say something when they were interrupted by a short, sharp cry. Ross turned, trying to determine where the sound came from. "Al?" he asked.

"Al? Who's Al?"

But Ross bolted from the room as another sobbing cry came, this one clearly from the kitchen.

Lisa hesitated only for a moment. Then she turned and pulled out the drawer. Tucked into the corner was a tiny key. Grabbing it, she shoved it into her pocket before following Ross to find out what happened.

She skidded into the kitchen to find her mother doubled up on the floor, with Ross kneeling over her. It looked like he was trying to take her pulse, or help her up, or something. She couldn't tell.

She couldn't even move. The sight of her mother, thrashing into a tighter and tighter knot as if somebody had stabbed her in the gut, making noises like a hurt kitten, paralyzed her. Her mother's skirt had rucked up along her thigh, and Lisa saw without really seeing as Ross smoothed it down to a decent length, and then had to do it again as Jenniver twisted under his hands.

She had kicked one shoe off, and it had come to rest against one leg of the kitchen table, the laces still tied, a plain taupe loafer. One of a pair that she'd always thought of as her mother's "sensible shoes." The laces on the other shoe, oddly, had come loose, and whipped against the floor where her feet churned up and down. There was a terrible smell in the air.

Ross looked up, yelled something at her, and she stepped back, away from the desperation in his eyes. He yelled again, and the words finally made sense to her. "Call an ambulance! Get help!"

Help. Yes. It broke her paralysis, allowed her to turn her back on the two of them, to shut out the sight of them. She couldn't shut out the sound, though, and held one hand over her free ear as she dialed 911 and tried to make the report. The mewling got quieter and quieter, and if it weren't for the steady, reassuring murmur of Ross's voice that never stopped, never stopped for a moment, she would have turned back to look and see if her mother was dying.

But Ross kept talking, reassuring both her and her mother, and she didn't have to look. She kept the phone at her ear even after the line disconnected so she wouldn't have to turn around and see. Her fingers, pressing hard on their own sweat, slipped against the plastic.

She had to hang up, at last, when the disconnect signal began hammering in her ear. By that time her mother was almost quiet, except for the rasp of her breathing, and Lisa risked turning again.

"Get me a wet hand towel," Ross said. It took Lisa a moment to realize that though the words were still in that steady, quiet voice, he was talking to her now, not her mother. "Soak it in cold water, the coldest you can get, and wring it out. Come on, Lisa, move it. Now!"

Her mother's hand was clinging to his, making white dents that had to hurt, but he wasn't trying to get loose. He remained where he was, kneeling beside her, holding her hand, his arm around her so that she wasn't lying on the floor any more but was supported on his lap. Her eyes were squeezed shut, her lips parted as she panted.

"Lisa," Ross said. Once again his voice broke her paralysis, and she ran for the linen cabinet.

By the time she had run the water, soaked and wrung out the towel, and brought it back to him, she could hear the sirens approaching. Ross was holding it to her mother's face, patting her forehead and cheeks and holding it to her eyes, when the paramedics rang the doorbell. Then there was nothing but confusion, with the gurney and the people milling around in the kitchen. Finally Ross had to help them lift her mother, taking most of her weight himself, and lower her to the cot. Jenniver screamed again as she was moved, and Ross was there to talk to her, to hold her hand. Lisa had never thought that

Ross, wiry and tough as he might be, would have had the strength to hold her mother steady until she was lying straight and the straps were on her, holding her securely in place.

The telephone rang in the midst of things, and she went to answer it and ran out into the front yard as they were loading the gurney into the ambulance.

"Ross! It's Daddy! He wants you to pick him up at the hotel!"

Ross swung around to say something, and Jenniver reached for him again. Ross disengaged his arm and placed her hand down again, spoke to her, and came over to Lisa. Lisa could see her mother staring after Ross, a look of loss and terror in her eyes. The red and blue lights laid stripes of color across her pale face. Neighbors gathered on the sidewalk and chattered to each other, making no move to come closer and find out what was going on.

"Is your dad still on the line?" he said, putting his hands on her shoulders. She nodded, grateful for the support. "Do you want to go to the hospital?"

She nodded again. "What's wrong with her?" Her voice surprised her. She thought it would be stronger than that.

"They don't know yet," he said. He didn't say that *he* didn't know, though, and he looked as if he would cry, if men did that kind of thing. He swallowed. "They've got to run a bunch of tests."

"Is she going to be all right?" She almost yelped at the reflexive tightening of his hands.

"They don't know yet," he repeated. "I've got to talk to your dad." Then he was gone, back into the house, and she was left standing in the slanting shade of the cottonwood tree, one hand on its bark to anchor her to reality, watching them close the ambulance doors, watching the drivers get in and pull away from the curb, the vehicle go down the street and turn the corner and disappear from sight, lights flashing.

The neighbors didn't approach her. They looked uneasily at her, and they looked down the now-empty street, and one by one they went away, back into their houses and cars, until she was the only one left in the slanting sunlight of the setting sun. The tree bark crumbled under her fingers, and she wondered why she no longer felt like crying. She no longer felt like anything at all.

She couldn't shake the feeling that there was still someone watching her sympathetically, and she looked around but there was no one there. Shuddering, she stuffed her fists into her pockets and went back to the house herself, fingering the tiny key from her father's desk.

"I don't understand why you couldn't have told me," her father said in a querulous tone. "I shouldn't have to hear about this from Ross. Couldn't you have told me your mother was sick?"

Lisa stared out the window and said nothing. Ross, sipping a paper cup of coffee across the room, didn't appear to be paying any attention; his head was tilted as if he was listening to something else anyway.

Ross was acting awfully weird these days. But it was probably a good thing, because the Ross from before wouldn't have held on to her mom that way.

"Dammit, listen to me!"

This time her father's frustrated outburst got Ross's attention as well as her own. Ross came over and stood beside her.

"Dr. Wales—"

"Shut up, Ross. I'm talking to my daughter here."

Lisa shrugged and looked away.

"I asked you a question!"

"I dunno," she said.

The three of them were alone in the waiting room, a small alcove off the end of the hall. Large windows overlooked the city, showing the lights as a wash of jewels against the darkness. The north-south freeway was a river of light, the Saturday-night traffic to and from uptown and Santa Fe getting heavier as the hour got later. A four-foot-wide orange stripe made a horizontal band around the walls of the room, separating slate blue on the bottom from muted yellow on top. The ceiling was plain white acoustical tile, the linoleum of the floor was battleship gray. The couches were in shades of orange and rust and brown and cream. The coffee machine was old and dented. A small table held a half-assembled jigsaw puzzle. The room looked as if the hospital had run out of money for the decorator halfway through.

"You're not paying attention to me, are you?" Stephen Wales said.

Lisa stared at the floor.

"I shouldn't have to find out your mother's sick from a stranger!" He was shouting now, and Lisa glanced sideways at Ross, hoping he'd say something. But being called a stranger had shut him up, at least for the moment. He was staring at her father but not saying a word.

"You could've seen she was sick if you ever paid attention," she said at last.

Wales raised his hand. Ross moved at last, not much, but somehow his shoulder was between her

162

father's hand and herself. Her father looked at him, anger red in his face. "Get out of my way."

"Calm down." Ross sounded older. He had more authority in his voice than her father did, mad as he was.

"Don't tell me how to handle my daughter." He reached out to shove Ross aside. Ross didn't move.

"This isn't how to handle anybody. Calm down," Ross repeated.

"This is a family matter. It's none of your business." But he dropped his hand, and Ross backed off. Not much, but a little bit. "I paid attention, young lady. She never said the first thing to me about being sick. Are you saying she told you?"

"She didn't have to. I could tell just by looking at her. You never even looked at her."

"What—"

But Lisa was tired of being quiet. "You ate your dinner and got up and went into your office and closed the door and never even looked at her. You went to all your group meetings and never asked how she was feeling. She's been feeling bad for weeks and weeks, and you never even noticed!"

"Lisa!"

She dodged around a nurse, who glared at her father and made shushing noises, and ran into the hall, toward the nursing station. She only got halfway there before Ross caught up with her.

"Lisa, wait—"

"What for? So he can yell at me? He can stand there so self-righteous about how she never said anything, and so he's not to blame!"

"Lisa, *nobody's* 'to blame' that your mom is sick. It isn't anything he did or you did. It just happened.

163

But your father needs you now—"

"Yeah, sure," she snarled. "That's why he's yelling at me. He doesn't need me. He doesn't need anybody."

They had to lower their voices when one of the patients got up out of bed and closed a door, hard.

"He does need you," Ross insisted. "He's scared. He doesn't know how to say it. Look, your mother is in there with all those doctors and he hasn't even had a chance to see her yet. At least you got to see her. Give him a break, okay?"

"Why should I? He never gives me one."

"You're acting damned childish," he snapped.

"Maybe because I'm a kid!" she snapped back.

He bit back a response, took a deep breath. "Okay. I deserve that." He looked up the hallway to the waiting room. Her father wasn't visible. "Look, I'm going to talk to the doctor. They won't let you in to see her if she goes into the ICU anyway, you're not sixteen yet—"

"Next month!" she protested.

"I know—"

"We could just tell them!"

He took another deep breath, and his gaze slid to one side and he was quiet a minute. "I can't lie," he said, as if to somebody else.

"It isn't a lie. I'm *practically* sixteen, and it's a dumb rule anyway."

He looked exasperated, but not at her. He shook his head. "I know it's arbitrary—"

"Say what?"

He blinked and looked at her. "Arbitrary. Ah, determined by whim or caprice. Based on or subject to individual judgment or discretion."

"Huh? You sound like some dictionary. What does that mean?"

"It means," he said, looking daggers over her shoulder, "that they just decided sixteen was the right age for no good reason."

"Well then," she said, "can't we just decide fifteen's a good age too?"

"It's their hospital," he said feebly.

"It's my mother."

His face twisted, as if she, or someone, had said "Gotcha."

"Look, I'll see what I can do. I'll find out how she is, talk to the doctor. I can't promise anything."

"I don't want to wait."

"Part of growing up is learning how to wait," he said. Then, for no good reason, he added, "Yeah, that's why you never grew up."

"What?" she said. But by that time she was talking to his back as he headed to the nursing station. She drew a deep breath and held it, unconsciously, but somehow, watching his back, she felt suddenly comforted, as if someone who wasn't really there had given her a hug.

CHAPTER

SIXTEEN

Al was reviewing, for no particular reason, a part of the download for the year 1968. A running text at the top of the screen supplemented the microscreen visual of a television news clip: Robert Kennedy in the Ambassador Hotel, brushing at his hair, raising one hand in victory, proclaiming, "On to Chicago!"

"Freeze," Al commanded. Ziggy obediently froze the picture on the famous grin. Al continued to stare at it. He had been there, in that audience. He had seen that smile. Here, more than thirty years later, he could freeze the moment, prevent the candidate from leaving the stage and going through the corridor that led to the hotel kitchen and an assassin's bullets.

"Summarize the vote in the California primary."

A graphic replaced the freeze-frame. Al shook his head, chewed on his unlit cigar.

"Summarize the national election."

"Why?" Ziggy asked, as the graph melted and re-formed to reflect the November 1968 results. "You are exhibiting displacement activity, Admiral Calavicci."

"What do you mean, 'displacement activity'? I happen to be interested in this period."

"But the 1968 national elections are not related to Dr. Beckett's current Leap. You're supposed to be researching the Wales family."

"Well, do you have any more information about Dr. Beckett's current Leap?" Al challenged.

Ziggy scanned his databases. "No," the computer admitted.

"I like that sulky tone of voice. Was that Sam's idea, or Tina's?" When the computer didn't respond, he went on, "Tina's, I'll bet. Sam doesn't know how to sulk. He goes out and *does* things."

"As you did, in the summer of 1968, before you went to Vietnam. That completes my data arc. I understand now. You are trying to re-create the sense of accomplishment that you lacked ten years ago, in the moment that Dr. Beckett is experiencing now."

"Are we going to start calling you 'Dr. Ziggy'?" Al snarled. "Did you get programmed with a degree in psychology while I was gone?" He swung his feet off the desk. "Whaddaya mean, I lacked a sense of accomplishment? I accomplished a lot. A hell of a lot."

"You had accomplished a great deal by the time you retired in 1990," the computer agreed. "But at that particular point you were at a cusp, similar to the decision points to which Dr. Beckett has Leaped in the past."

"But we don't *want* him to change things for me!" Al protested. "I want to end up exactly where I am. I don't want him changing anything."

"It may be that in order for you to end up exactly where you are, Dr. Beckett has to change where you were then."

Al knit his brows, thinking about this. "That would mean that the past that Dr. Beck——that Sam's in now"— cigar jabbed the air—"is a different past than the present"— the cigar moved a foot to the right and punctuated the air again—"that we're in. Now."

"That's correct," Ziggy acknowledged.

"Then where's *our* past?" The cigar described a question-mark curve.

"If our speculation is correct, Dr. Beckett hasn't created it yet."

"That's silly. That's like building the top floor of a building before you build the foundation."

"That, too, is correct."

"So why haven't we fallen down?"

If a computer could shrug, Ziggy would have. "Perhaps for the same reason that Dr. Beckett started Leaping in the first place, Admiral. We have postulated that Dr. Beckett's Leaping, in which he changes the past, is necessary to bring about the future—his future—which enables our present to exist."

"Awww, c'mon." Al had had this conversation with the computer before, and it inevitably left him with a headache. "Look, we said before it doesn't matter, okay? Sam Leaps. Doesn't matter why, he Leaps. Sometime he's going to Leap back where he belongs, and stay, and this whole mess is going to be over with. So let's not start talking about him changing me, okay? I'm still the same lovable guy I always was, and I always will be. No changes. None."

Al marched upstairs to get supper in the minisized cafeteria provided for the Project staff, leaving the computer behind him, blinking in rainbow lights. "But change," Ziggy observed, to no one, "is essential."

No one answered.

The graphic on the screen melted back into the freeze-frame of Robert Kennedy, smiling and waving to his cheering supporters. The frame unfroze, and the camera followed the doomed candidate as he turned and exited through the door behind the stage, and down the hall, and into history.

Jenniver Wales looked almost as pale as the sheets she rested on. Stephen Wales stood at the foot of the bed, one hand on her foot, the other on the baseboard, and smiled widely. Too widely, Sam thought. It looked more like a rictus than an expression of happiness.

They had come to the desk, seeking directions, only to find that Jenniver was in the Emergency Room, that doctors were running tests, attempting to stabilize her, to determine what was wrong. An earnest-looking young intern, terribly tired, had overheard them and had whisked Stephen Wales aside for a consultation. Sam had distracted Lisa somehow. When Wales came back, he was pale. Sam had snagged the doctor himself as father and daughter went down the hall, and represented himself shamelessly as a relative to find out what tests were being run. Sometime later, the immediate crisis abated, Jenniver had been checked into a room on an upper floor.

Lisa, for her part, was as close to her mother as she could get without actually sitting on the bed. She'd tried, but Sam, haunted by flashes of senior nurses skilled at intimidating even genius interns, had shooed her off. Now she held her mother's fingers as if they were brittle sticks that might break if she exerted too much pressure.

The tape holding the I.V. needle in place on the top of Jenniver's hand didn't quite hide the bruising from repeated needle jabs. Sam had gritted his teeth and reminded himself that even if he was a doctor, he probably couldn't have done any better. Jenniver didn't appear to mind, and the metal pole suspending the I.V. bag was shoved back into a corner, out of the way. A heart monitor beeped softly in the background, to the rhythm of a blinking light.

"You gave us quite a scare," Wales was saying. "But they said . . . they said you're okay, really, you'll be back home. Maybe . . . maybe even tomorrow." His teeth showed. "There's all those dirty dishes in the sink, you know." He was trying to make a joke.

Jenniver looked at him and said nothing.

Sam, standing in the doorway, trying not to intrude on the family, knew that look. He'd seen it before.

His own father had that look. A dozen, a hundred patients had that look. It was patience. Endurance. Fatalism.

It might not last; there were stages that people were supposed to go through: anger, denial, bargaining, depression, acceptance. The doctor had rattled off words to him, not expecting that a college student only nineteen years old would understand. Ross Malachy probably wouldn't have understood, probably would have nodded and acted as if the medical

171

gobbledygook all made sense.

But Sam Beckett, M. among other Ds, did understand, and it did make sense. He might not be able to recall large pieces of his medical education, but he knew the kind of tests that were run when the suspected diagnosis was second-stage ovarian cancer. Al was right, as much as he hated to admit it; Jenniver was beyond helping. Even if he had hauled her off to the hospital the very first second he'd ever laid eyes on her, it wouldn't have made a difference.

The difference had to be in her husband and daughter. Stephen Wales *was* exhibiting the classic symptoms of denial.

"You'll have to take a couple of days off, I guess," he said. "Get your strength back—"

Jenniver closed her eyes.

"Why don't you just shut up, Daddy?" Lisa said.

Jenniver winced. The man jerked as if the words had slapped him. "Don't you talk to me that way!"

Lisa didn't answer. Instead, she leaned forward and kissed her mother on the forehead, whispering something that only she could hear. She placed her mother's bandaged hand on the sheet and moved away, past Sam and out the door, never looking back.

Sam turned to go after her, but Wales stumbled out as if following. Sam cast one last look at Jenniver, whose eyes were open again. Her lips curved, and she nodded, giving him permission to go.

The three of them drove back to the house in silence. Wales walked into the kitchen and looked around at the sink, now half-full of cold gray water, a thin rim of soap bubbles still clinging to the inner edge of the plates. Jenniver had fixed sandwiches for supper for herself and Ross and Lisa; the mustard was still open on the kitchen table. Sam moved automatically to close the jar and put it away.

"Don't," Wales said. "That's Lisa's job. Lisa, get in here!"

"I'll do it." Sam continued to tidy up.

"You shouldn't be doing this," Wales insisted. "She's got to learn she's got chores around here."

"It's late, and her mother's in the hospital, and she doesn't know for sure how bad it is yet. She's worried and upset and scared." Sam drained the dirty dish water, started refilling the sink with hot. "I think she can let the kitchen go this once. I'll do it, okay?"

"No, it isn't okay! Self-discipline means doing things even when they're hard to do. Lisa, get in here!"

But he didn't address the reference to Jenniver, Sam noted. For a man so concerned about the capacity of men to get in touch with their identities and emotions, he seemed to be missing something essential about the other half of the human race—for instance, the fact that their emotions were legitimate, too.

From the back of the house came the sound of Guns 'N Roses at high decibels.

"I'm going to take that damned CD player and throw it in the garbage—"

Sam, whose taste ran more to show tunes, privately agreed, but wiped his hands on a dish towel. "I'll go talk to her."

"I could talk to my own daughter," Wales grumbled, but he made no move to stop Sam.

At least she'd closed her door. Sam paused, screwing up his courage; the door panel was fairly vibrating with the bass line.

There was only one way to deal with it. He opened the door, spotted the console, and strode over to hit the off button.

The silence was nearly as deafening as the noise.

Lisa was sprawled face down on the bed, her ears protected by pillows wrapped in place by her arms.

Sam sat beside her, tugging one arm loose. "Lisa?"

She hauled the pillow back into place.

He wasn't going to let her get away with it. This time he pulled both arms away and tossed the pillows across the room. "Lisa."

She twisted around, her T-shirt riding up almost to her bra line, exposing tanned ribs. "You shut off my CD."

"Yeah. Your dad wanted to throw it away."

"He keeps saying that, but he never does it."

"This time I think he meant it." He looked around the room, realized he was sitting on the bed, very close to her, and got up hastily.

Posters of rock stars decorated the sliding closet doors. A garland of dusty paper flowers draped the corner of a mirror. Photographs were stuck haphazardly in the mirror frame. The bedspread was a handmade patchwork quilt; the floor was covered by a rag rug. Lisa's furniture was battered and scarred and lovingly polished.

"My mother's gonna die, isn't she?" Lisa said, sitting up and pulling her shirt back into place. Sam let out a small unconscious sigh of relief, and then her question hit him. He swallowed.

"Yes, she's going to die."

Her eyes were wide and dry, and her fingers clenched a pink satin square on the quilt. "No."

"Yes, Lisa. Not tonight, I don't mean she's going to die tonight." He would have given anything to take away the look on her face, anything but a lie. "But she's going to die. We don't know enough to save her."

"But she's in the hospital. They're doctors. They're supposed to know."

"They're doctors, sure, but they're not gods. They're people. It's ovarian cancer, and we just don't know enough."

She was quiet again, her fingers working back and forth. "How—how long does she have to live?"

Her voice was breaking, and Sam wanted to turn away, to give the tears forming in her eyes the dignity of privacy, but he couldn't. Maybe, he thought, because his urge to turn away didn't have enough to do with her dignity, and too much with his.

"I don't know for sure. It depends on how well she responds to radiation therapy. How much she wants to live. She needs you, Lisa."

"*I* need *her*," she said. "It's not fair."

"No. It isn't fair." He didn't say, *Life isn't fair*. She knew that as well as he did.

"I don't want her to die!" she burst out.

Anger. Denial. Bargaining. Depression. Acceptance. He ran over the stages in his mind, not sure he had them right, not sure they were in the right order. But there they were, the recognized stages in dealing with grief, psychologically appropriate responses.

And his own distancing, attempting to turn her pain into chapters from a textbook, that was denial, too, and it wouldn't help her one bit to explain that what she was feeling was outlined and explained and all the best people in the field agreed that she was demonstrating the classic symptoms of emotional shock.

"Your dad needs you too, Lisa."

"He does *not*," she said. "He needs somebody to clean up the kitchen."

"Your father doesn't know how to deal with it either. He thinks that if everything looks normal, then things will *be* normal."

"He doesn't care."

"He *does* care. He cares a lot. He just doesn't know how to show it." Sam wished that Wales could invite his daughter—and his wife—to one of the encounter sessions he ran, just so his own family could see him in a different light. It was crazy how the man could be so nurturing to strangers and never realize how coldly he was behaving to his own family. Perhaps the difference was that in the encounter group he felt in control of things.

"I thought that was his whole thing, how to show his feelings. Isn't that what you guys do in those meetings of yours? How can you say he doesn't know how? He just doesn't feel anything, that's all."

The Door slid open, and Al walked into the middle of the bed, looked over at the girl, and saying "Excuse me," stepped to one side, so that he was "standing" on the rug.

Sam looked at him. Al shook his head.

"It won't help your mother if you give your father problems. This is going to be a bad time for your whole family. The best thing you can do is help your father." It sounded very much like a platitude, even to him. Al stood by, unusually somber.

"Bullshit." But her heart wasn't in it. She shook her head. "You really think—"

And at that moment the door crashed open, and Stephen Wales stood in the open doorway, his face red. "How many times have I told you to keep this door open?" he shouted. "I've been calling you!"

"Hey—" Sam began.

Wales turned on him. "And what the hell were you doing back here with my daughter? You were supposed to tell her to turn off that damned record player, not stay back here in her bedroom!"

"Don't argue with him, Sam," Al said.

Sam wasn't about to argue with him. He raised his hands and went past the furious father and out the door, trying not to hear the raised voices behind him.

"Well, whaddaya know. I didn't think you'd have the good sense to get out of there," Al remarked, floating along at his side.

"What was I supposed to do? I could only make things worse." He let himself out the kitchen door and went up the outside stairs to the apartment over the garage. "Al, I don't know *what* I'm supposed to do here."

He sagged down on the couch, holding his head in his hands. "I really don't know. If I thought he was going to hit her, I could have stopped him. But what am I supposed to do? I can't save Jenniver. I thought I could, maybe, but if the cancer has already metastasized, there's no way. She's going to die, and nothing I can do will stop that. As for Lisa—"

He shook his head. "Al, what am I supposed to do?"

"Make it right," Al said. "Fix it, and Leap."

"I don't think it's fixable," Sam said, looking down at Ross Malachy's pale long-fingered hands, twisting together before him. "I don't think I can make this one right. I don't know what to do."

"Well, one thing you can do is ask her what she's planning to do with Stenno and a gun tomorrow night," Al informed him. "Get up off your butt, mister. You're not done yet. You have work to do."

CHAPTER

SEVENTEEN

Stenno lay curled up in the dark, holding the phone away from his ear as Lisa sobbed. From time to time he made reassuring noises, in between swigs from a beer bottle. Most of his attention was on the heavy metal music video on the TV in front of him. He had gathered that Lisa's mother was in the hospital, that she was going to die. What a shame. . . . He had more important things on his mind.

"Did you get the gun?" he asked, when it sounded as if the girl on the other end of the line had calmed down.

"No," she whimpered. "I got the key to the cabinet, but—"

"Hey, I told you to get the gun!" The voice on the other end filled up with sobs again, and he changed tactics instantly. "C'mon, baby, I know it's hard for you. Shit, you've had a lot of things happen tonight! And your dad's being a real asshole, isn't he?"

Affirmative sniffles.

"I keep telling you, baby, you don't have to take that shit. All you have to do is take the gun out of the cabinet and hide it, and that'll put a scare into him. Put it in that lilac bush. You know the one. He'll never find it there.

"C'mon, baby, you can do this. You're my woman, right?" The video changed to a country-western tune he liked. He turned up the volume a notch.

More sniffles, uncertain.

"Sure you are, baby. And my woman is strong, man. She doesn't sit and cry like some baby. She *does* things.

"And you're gonna prove that your father doesn't own the whole universe. He's gonna come in and find that thing gone, and man, he's gonna shit bricks. And you're gonna be the only one who knows where it went! Right? You think about that." He was pouring it on thick now, keeping one eye on the screen. He wanted to get this conversation over with so he could at least hear the end of the song.

"You think about that bastard standing there like nothing in the world's going on, while your mom's in the hospital. Telling you to do the dishes like you're his servant or something. He can't tell you what to do."

"He'll call the cops," she objected.

"No he won't. Hey, it's gonna take him a couple of days to notice, right? And he won't know how long it's been gone. Maybe he'll even think you took it!"

Now her voice was filled with alarm. "He'll get mad!"

"But he can't do anything about it! He won't know for sure! See, all you have to do is say you don't

know anything about it. And maybe he'll think"—
Stenno was chuckling now—"that you still have it
and you're gonna blow him away. Guess that'll make
him respectful, huh?"

A silence on the other end of the line showed that
Lisa was considering this, visualizing the scene,
thinking about her father looking at her as a person,
a strong person, a person with a gun. She couldn't see
herself as a person with a gun. Neither could Stenno,
but that was beside the point. She had access to a
gun, and that was what counted.

"You are my strong woman," he crooned. "My cool
woman. Your daddy thinks he knows about head
games? He doesn't know shit about the head games
you're gonna play on him. He's gonna think he's
going crazy. And he deserves it. Doesn't he? The
way he acts. You wouldn't have to do this to him
if he was acting right, would you?"

"No," she said hesitantly.

"It's his fault," Stenno whispered. "His fault.
You have to teach him. You're gonna take it and
hide it. And you'll take other things and hide
them"— mustn't let the girl think the gun was
the point of it all—"and he's going to think he's
gone nuts. You have the key. Why wait? Do it
tonight. Take it out tonight and hide it in the
lilac bush. You'll know where it is and he won't.
My strong woman."

"Yeah," Lisa said. The tears were almost gone
now. "Yeah! I can go after he goes to bed. I'll
do it."

"Good girl. I tell you what, I'll come and wait outside, so if he gives you any grief I'll be right there,
okay?"

"Really?" The idea that she would have some support, however invisible, was a great relief. "That would be cool. I'll do it."

Stenno grinned. "I knew you would. Okay, but be cool now, okay? Don't let him suspect anything. Stay cool."

"Okay." A pause, as if she were looking around. "I love you, Stenno."

A grimace crossed his face like a shadow. "Me too," he responded. She didn't notice his lack of enthusiasm. With a quick kissing noise, the line disconnected.

The video ended at the same time. Swearing, Stenno got up, took a last swig of his beer. Lisa was as screwed up as her father was. He couldn't depend on her for shit. Oh, she'd get the gun, if she thought he was out there. But he had no intention of waiting around the Wales house in the dark for whenever she found the guts to get the damned thing. He could always pick it up in the morning.

Maybe he'd better go back one more time and check things out at the mall. Just to see what was going on. How many cops were around. That kind of thing. And maybe find somebody with some good shit to help him sleep tonight. He'd want to be rested and ready tomorrow.

It never hurt to be prepared.

The soon-to-be-ex-Admiral Calavicci ran at a steady, no-nonsense pace, avoiding the darker shadows of potholes and ripped-up asphalt as if they weren't there. He was wearing a navy-blue-and-white warm-up suit, and for once there was no cigar in his hand.

Time was he would have killed an evening in a bar, drinking alone if he had no buddies, flirting like crazy with the barmaids, finding company somehow. But he hadn't had a drink in a while. He didn't need it somehow, not like before.

He was one of the lucky ones and he knew it. He wasn't an alcoholic. He could, if he wanted, take a drink and stop for the night, for the week, for the month. He used to get drunk when things got too bad, but he'd had a friend who helped him see how dumb that was, and he didn't get drunk any more.

Now, when he was lonely and in a strange city, he ran.

There were quite a few runners around the mall parking lot. It was well lighted—well, most of it was, though the south side did leave something to be desired—and in fairly good shape. Enough people did this that the city had provided measurements of the circumference. Two miles around the outermost perimeter, along two heavily traveled streets and then behind the restaurants and the multiplex movie theater, out again beside another, less well traveled road.

He hated running. He hated wheezing and panting, and the process of getting warmed up, the stretching exercises, seemed damned silly for a man his age. But the running allowed him to eat what he wanted, and he had to admit that his stamina for other, more pleasurable activities had increased amazingly. That alone made it worth while. And it didn't hurt his own attractiveness any, either.

So he wheezed and panted and made himself run, using the iron discipline that had kept him alive for years as a POW. As he ran he counted the cars in the mall parking lot, comparing totals as he made his circuits. When he had started tonight's run the mall was still open and the lot was full. Now only the Saturday night after-the-movie restaurant crowd lingered. The usual collection of trucks and minivans and sedans, a couple of upscale BMWs, and one very nice silver Jag were scattered near the restaurant entrances.

On his last circuit, most of the vehicles were gone. He looked for the Jag; its owner too had either called it a night or gone out to the bars and dance clubs, looking for whatever excitement Albuquerque had to offer at this time of the evening. In its place was an old VW van, rusty red over cream. Al noted it, wondered why anybody would come to a closed mall. He had the feeling that he had seen that particular van somewhere else, and recently. He thought about it as he ran. Cream and rust—yeah. That kid who had been giving what's-his-name, Malachy, a hard time this afternoon had been driving a cream-and-rust VW van.

There wasn't any law against punks parking in mall lots late in the evening, though. He forgot about it in the effort to make that last half mile back to the hotel room and a hot shower.

Sam was finding it difficult to sleep. Al had dropped his bombshell and looked at the handlink and gone away without another word. There had to be some word beyond maddening for this kind of behavior.

He knew Lisa was going to be involved in a robbery in a mall tomorrow, but precisely when and where, not even pacing back and forth could tell him. He kept going back to the window and looking down at the front door where Lisa had stood, crying for admittance at a locked door. No one stood there now, of course; Lisa and her father had long since gone to bed, the house was quiet. Even the traffic on Central had died away. There were crickets, of course. Cicadas. Wind in the cottonwoods.

He found himself longing for very loud Guns 'N Roses again. Anything to disrupt the deceptive peacefulness of the summer night. "Al, where are you when I need you?" he muttered.

"Right here." Al appeared out of the wall.

Sam jumped. "Where's the Door?"

"Out on the steps. Well, where I came in was on the steps." He poked at the handlink, and the Door slid upward behind him, revealing a solid glow. "See? Door."

Sam squinted. "Okay, okay. Door. Now are you going to explain that business about the gun? What gun?"

Al sighed. "The gun belonging to Stephen Wales which was used in the mall robbery tomorrow. Was used? Will be used? Leaping is hell on the tenses."

"How come you went flaming out of here like that?"

"Ziggy found a way to get into the closed files. The robbery happens—happened—about ten minutes before closing."

"Where in the mall?" Sam said through clenched teeth.

Al raised bushy eyebrows, continued with elaborate patience. "A store called Nora's Notions. Lisa and her boyfriend—"

"Stenno."

"Yeah, Stenno." Al, patience running out, looked annoyed at the interruption, but then he always looked annoyed when Sam already knew the answer. He slapped the handlink, just on general principles. "Lisa and Stenno came in. Stenno had the gun. An innocent bystander, there to get some rickrack—what the hell is rickrack?"

"It's a notion." Sam Beckett, genius, wasn't about to admit he didn't know either. "Go on."

"Okay, it's a notion. What's a notion?"

"Al!"

"Okay. The proprietor, a Mrs. Lily Sanchez, got in the way. Caught a bullet. Died of it. Stenno was tried as an adult. Lisa went into the juvenile system. You know the rest."

Sam took a deep breath. "So I need to prevent Lisa from getting involved in this robbery."

"It would be nice if Mrs. Sanchez survived, too," Al observed.

Sam glared at him. "When is Ziggy going to start functioning like he's supposed to? When am I going to Leap somewhere and get all the information I need, the *right* information, the first time? Hasn't anybody on that Project ever heard of a quality initiative?"

Al winced. "Hey, Ziggy was *your* baby. *Your* design."

"Oh, great. So this whole thing is my fault."

"Well, maybe not. But you gotta remember it's tough to pick the right data out. I mean, we've talked about this before."

Sam closed his eyes and summoned patience. "Let's get back to the point. The gun, Al. How does Stephen Wales's gun get to Stenno?"

Al looked at him incredulously. "Not even you are that naive, Sam. Lisa gave it to him. Obviously."

"Obviously." Sam was finding it difficult to talk through gritted teeth. "When?"

"Oh." Al checked the handlink. "Oh. Um. We don't seem to have that information."

"You. Don't. Seem. To. Have. That. Information.

"So help me, I'm going to Leap back there just to kick that computer—"

The handlink squealed, and Al patted it anxiously. "Don't hurt his feelings, Sam."

"It's a computer, for crying out loud—"

"You gave it feelings."

"Yeah, right." He turned away from the hologram to look out the window again. "Okay. At least we know what, where, and when. I guess how isn't all that important. I wish I knew why, though. I tried to tell her that her parents really needed her now most of all, and I thought she was listening."

"During the psychiatric hearings she said she did it to hurt her father."

"To *hurt* her father—" Sam turned back. "How can he be hurt any more than he is already?"

"She doesn't see it. He's busy doing his masculinism thing and keeping his feelings to himself, and she doesn't see it."

"But that's not what it's all about! That whole men's movement was supposed to be about knowing when you're angry, or happy, or hurting, or whatever it is you're feeling. And recognizing when other people are feeling those things. Not this idiotic 'keeping his feelings to himself'. . . ." Exasperated, he swung away from the hologram to stare out the window again.

Al couldn't quite bring himself to look up, not even to face the back of Sam's head. "Not everybody is as enlightened about that stuff as you are, Sam."

" 'Enlightened'?"

"I wish you'd stop quoting me," Al muttered.

"I wish I knew what was going on down there right now," Sam muttered.

"What?" Al edged up beside him, unwittingly linking arms, to peer out the window. "You mean. . . . Uh-oh."

"Uh-oh," Sam agreed. The two men watched as lights blinked on, then off, from the living room to the dining room. And then a fainter light, reflected from down the hall, as a light in one of the back rooms came on, remained on for several minutes. Then the light blinked off, on, off, on, off, in a deliberate pattern.

And the order of lights reversed itself, as someone moved back through the house, back to the bedroom wing, whatever needed to be done, accomplished. Sam didn't need to be told that the blinking light had been a signal. The only person in that house who would be signaling was Lisa, sending some message to her boyfriend, who was probably out there in the dark somewhere, watching.

But what was she signaling? What had Lisa done?

CHAPTER

EIGHTEEN

"We're going to have another group meeting this afternoon," Wales announced the next morning. He was dressed in a three-piece suit and tie, looking uncertainly back and forth from the toaster to a loaf of unsliced bread. "I spoke to the hotel people, and we can get the room. Some of the men decided they needed another storytelling."

"A storytelling?" Sam was feeling remarkably stupid, but at least he could cope with toast and jelly. He took the loaf and rummaged in the drawer for a bread knife. "When exactly is this going to happen, and aren't you going back to the hospital?"

Wales cleared his throat, took off his glasses and made a production of polishing them, peering at the lenses, and polishing them again. "There's nothing I can do at the hospital. They're going to be running more tests and things. I've set this up for four o'clock this afternoon. You'll have to take me over to the hotel, of course."

"Four o'clock?" He really was repeating things. Al was right. He was turning into a regular echo chamber. "What time does the mall close?"

"Five o'clock on Sundays," Lisa answered. She was wearing an old, oversized navy blue work shirt, tight blue jeans, and new sandals, and she sat on a stool and spun around, snatching an untoasted slice of bread out of Sam's hand and nibbling away the crust, steadily filling her mouth without swallowing. "How come?" she mumbled.

"I was going to pick up a couple of things," Sam improvised. He caught the toast as it popped up, spread a minimum of butter on it, and slapped grape jelly on top of it. Stephen Wales held out a plate. Sam gave the toast away and started more for himself. "I was planning to go before it closed."

"Well, you'll just have to go earlier," Wales said. "I'll need you for the meeting. I've called all the group members already this morning. They're expecting me."

Sam nodded, keeping one eye on Lisa. She finished the crust and squeezed the middle of the slice into a ball of dough and bit a chunk out of it. "Actually, I was planning to go back to the hospital and see Mrs. Wales. How about it, Lisa? Are you coming? You could bring her some of her things."

She swallowed and took another bite, going to the refrigerator to pour out a large glass of orange juice. "They wouldn't let me see her unless you were there to talk them into it," she said. "So I don't see why I should go."

"I'm sure they'll let you in now that she's in a regular room. In fact, I could take you both over there this morning," he offered. "I'm sure she'd like to see you."

"I've already made up my mind," Wales announced. "I'm going to spend the morning working on the story-telling. I'll be in my office."

"You will?" Lisa's eyes sparkled.

"Yes, I will. Why?"

"No reason." Lisa bit into the ball of dough again, unsuccessfully hiding a smile.

Sam retrieved another pair of toast slices, only to lose them to Lisa. He carved more slices from the loaf.

"Needs more butter," Wales said.

"Butter's bad for you," Sam said automatically. "I'm sure that Jen—that Mrs. Wales would like to have some moral support today. She'd appreciate a visit."

"She'd appreciate getting the hospital bill paid, too," Wales said caustically.

"Is that why you're having this . . . storytelling thing?" Sam asked, pouring himself a glass of orange juice too and watching as Wales sat at the kitchen table, a linen place mat spread neatly before him, and wolfed down the toast. "Because you need to pay the hospital bill?"

"That's an unworthy remark. I'll take more toast, and pass the butter, please." He used the butter knife like a conductor's baton to spread a thick layer of animal fat and covered it with purple sugar. Sam, who had had his eye on the grape jelly himself, reconsidered and went back to slicing the loaf.

191

"What is a storytelling, anyway?" he asked. Seeing that neither Lisa nor her father had finished their last serving, he tore the most recent slices in half. He caught himself just short of repeating Lisa's trick of wadding the bread back into dough, and took a large mouthful. It was good bread.

"I assume you're asking this question in an effort to educate the child," Wales said. "Since you've done this at least a dozen times. We had one just yesterday, for heaven's sake."

Sam and Lisa both rolled their eyes, Lisa at the reference to herself as a "child," Sam at the reminder that there was still a lot about Ross Malachy's life that he didn't know. So that coming-of-age business had been a "storytelling"? "All right," he said, exaggerating his agreeableness just enough. "To educate the child."

Lisa snorted.

"It may not be appropriate to teach a female the secrets of our group."

This time Sam had to bite back his response. The bread was sticking in his throat. "The *secrets*?" he asked at last.

"Yeah, Daddy, tell me about your dumb secrets," Lisa chirped. "What do you do, bring in strippers?"

"That will be enough out of you, young lady." Wales placed the knife precisely across the plate. "I've told you before, you need to show respect."

"Yeah?" Lisa dipped her right index finger into the jelly jar, licked the purple glob off. Sam winced. "What are you gonna do, lock me out again?"

Her father's gaze remained fixed on the knife on his plate. "I'd like to remind you that your mother is not available to contravene my actions any longer."

For a moment Lisa looked frightened, then angry, then vindictive. "You know what? I think you're crazy. I think you guys get together and talk to each other because you can't find anybody else who wants to listen to you. I think you're all crazy, and one of these days they're going to come lock you up." She slid off the stool and faced her father, hands on her hips. "I think you're losing it. You're getting old and you're losing it, and you're just scared somebody's going to find out."

"Lisa," Sam said softly. "That's enough. Let's go to the hospital, okay? Let's go see your mom."

"She doesn't deserve to see her mother," Wales said.

"That's ridiculous." Sam had finally reached the end of his patience. "No matter what kind of a brat she's being—and you *are*," he informed her sharply, "no child 'doesn't deserve' to see her mother. Lisa, you need to straighten up. Go get your purse, or whatever. We're going to go to the hospital."

She huddled against the passenger-side door of the Blazer, staring out the window so she wouldn't have to talk to him as they drove. Sam didn't have to look at her as he talked; he was aware of her rejection of him, of the trip, of everything, as if she were a heat source trying to melt itself out through the side of the truck.

"Lisa, I know what you're planning," he began. "It's wrong. It isn't going to help anything."

"What are you talking about?"

She sounded so genuinely startled that he took advantage of a red light to glance over at her. "You know what I mean."

"No I don't." Her brows were knit in bewilderment. Then her expression changed, and she looked guilty.

"Yeah, you do. Lisa, how is what you're doing going to help your mother and father?"

"I don't care about my father. And it's not going to make any difference to my mom. They don't have anything to do with each other."

"Of course they do. They're your parents, they live together, they love each other."

Lisa laughed, a sharp ugly sound. "Love each other? Are you nuts? My dad only sees my mom at the dinner table, and most of the time he doesn't even look at her then. He eats and then he goes into his office and writes his articles, or he plays solitaire, or anything to keep from talking to her. He doesn't want to know anything about her. She's been sick for a long time, and he never even noticed. One time she fell, and her whole leg was bruised—it was black and blue from her toes to her hip—and he never even realized it.

"And she doesn't need him either. She's busy with her job and her garden and cooking and cleaning, and she never has anything to do with him. She wouldn't even tell him she felt bad. I think they only stay married to each other because she thinks divorce is a sin.

"So don't tell me anything *I* do matters."

Sam thought about this, and realized how much truth there was in her bitter words. "So, because they don't seem to love each other, you think they don't love you either?" The truck pulled into the parking lot, and he cruised a couple of aisles before spotting a place. Even on Sunday, it was

194

business as usual in a hospital, and the lot was packed.

"I don't know what love is," Lisa said flatly.

Sam shoved the gearshift into park. "You don't love anybody?"

"Nope," she said. Her voice was almost certain. She swallowed. "No."

"You don't love your mother? You don't care what happens to her?"

She opened her mouth to reply, closed it again. Then she said, "I don't love my dad. He doesn't care about me, and I don't care about him either."

He escorted her into the hospital, down the orange-striped halls and up the elevator to the wing where her mother waited, and didn't say a word. He couldn't think of anything to say. He knew better, he was certain that he knew better, but he couldn't think of any way on earth to convince Lisa that her assessment of her father was wrong.

Jenniver was sitting up this morning, and someone had loaned her cosmetics. The rouge was too bright for her, and the lipstick was the wrong color, but she greeted Sam and Lisa with a bright smile and patted the bed beside her, inviting her daughter to sit. Sam quelled his reflex and Lisa hopped up beside her mother. The woman in the next bed glared at them and got up, awkwardly, to pull the curtain between the two beds. The three of them listened to the other patient grunt her way back into bed and shared a wry smile.

Sam pulled up the single chair and sat at the end of the bed, listening to Jenniver and Lisa chatter awkwardly about makeup, and sneaked a look at the chart hanging from the footrail.

The tests had come back, all positive. Surgery was scheduled. It didn't surprise him. What did bother him was that Jenniver wasn't saying anything about it. Judging from her husband's behavior before breakfast and up until the time he and Lisa had left the house, he had no clue that his wife was going to undergo major surgery within the next few days. Surely the attending physician had called and spoken to Stephen? If so, the call must have come before Sam showed up for breakfast. But if he knew, why in God's name hadn't Wales come with them to the hospital? Didn't he want to be with his wife at a time like this?

Was Lisa right about how her parents felt about each other? She couldn't be, could she? Some knight-errant part of Sam Beckett's soul refused to believe that. The Wales family had problems, yes, but they couldn't be beyond redemption. Otherwise, what was the point of his Leaping into the situation?

Lisa was asking when Jenniver would be getting out.

"Oh, real soon now," Jenniver was saying. "They just want to check a couple of things."

Such as her liver and intestines, Sam thought. The indicated treatment was a total hysterectomy to remove the affected ovaries and the uterus, and a careful examination of other major organs to make sure that the cancer hadn't spread. According to Al, it already had, and the exploratory part of the surgery was going to find all kinds of trouble.

Lisa appeared to have forgotten, or chosen to ignore, what he had told her last night about her mother's dying. Maybe that was a blessing in disguise. But the doctors had to have told Jenniver

196

about the diagnosis, about the surgery. And she was acting like—she was actually telling her daughter—that she would be out of the hospital by tomorrow at the latest.

Nobody seemed to be dealing with the problem. He couldn't understand it. How could you solve a problem by ignoring it? He had never learned to stick his head in the ground and hope that troubles would go away, never learned to deal with other people who did.

Sam got up and excused himself and went down the hall, looking for horrible hospital coffee and a wisp of sanity to go.

And meanwhile, a battered cream-over-rust van pulled over to the curb around the corner and out of sight of the Wales house, and Stenno Baczek slid out of the driver's side and looked around. The streets were quiet; midday on a Sunday, most folks were in church. There weren't even any kids around riding their bikes. He smiled to himself.

Back yards in this part of town were divided by cinder block walls and lined with pyracantha or other greenery designed to discourage intruders. He didn't feel like getting his hands, or worse his new jacket, torn up. So he walked along as if he had every right in the world to be where he was, and turned the corner as if he knew exactly where he was going, and took the flagstone path along the side of the Wales house as if he lived there. The Blazer that Malachy drove was gone, he noticed; the sedan belonging to Mrs. Wales was still parked on the street.

Side yards were separated only by property dividers, sometimes only logs. The house next door to the

Waleses' had grass for a side yard; the Waleses had left theirs in ornamental rock, laid atop brittle black plastic. Once between houses and out of direct line of sight from the street, he allowed himself to relax. The only people who would see him now would have to be looking out the windows for him, and the only windows in the Wales house that overlooked this side were the bathroom and Lisa's bedroom. No one would be looking for him from those vantages; no one was likely to investigate the sound of fist-size pebbles crunching together under booted heels. He was safe.

The bathroom window, he noticed, had been cranked open. And the screen, torn in one corner, had been freshly taped down to prevent insects from entering. He grinned.

The blossoms on the lilac bush had long since turned brown. They needed to be trimmed back to allow new flowers next spring, but the only gardener in the family was otherwise occupied. The base of the lilac bush was cluttered with dead grasses, yellow and dried out, and the green of four-o'clocks that volunteered everywhere. Behind the lilac bush, where the dried grasses stood tall against the cracked stucco, there was a gap where something heavy rested. He pushed the lilac branches out of the way.

Yes. There, propped up against the wall as if someone had placed it there instead of dropping it from the window, rested a revolver. No sunlight could reach it here; there would be no betraying reflection from the stainless-steel barrel and frame. Stenno took it up and stood for a moment, admiring the weight of it in his hand. He pushed the barrel release, and the cylinder swung out. The gun was loaded.

It wasn't the automatic he had hoped for, but on the other hand, bullets were a bonus he never expected. He pushed at the ejector rod, and the bullets tumbled into and past his hands, yellow- and copper- and blue-tipped, scattering among the rocks and weeds. Within the house, he could hear the bathroom door opening, and he ducked down, swearing, scrambling for the ammunition, being as quiet as he could. The sounds of bathroom use covered his actions, but then the window began to creak above his head, and he pressed himself against the wall underneath. If the person closing the window chose to look outside, he would be found instantly. . . .

The window closed, and he stuffed the revolver under his jacket, cradling his arm to hold it, and ran, heedless of the rocks flying and the single blue-tipped bullet left gleaming in the sunlight behind him.

CHAPTER

NINETEEN

"Ziggy, play it again."

The only data available on the robbery/murder was from newspaper and TV news accounts of the incident, and the court records. It wasn't the kind of incident that commanded a great deal of attention, unless you were unfortunate enough to be involved; while murders didn't quite happen every day in Albuquerque, they came along often enough to make most news-hungry citizens skim the meager paragraphs quickly and move on to more momentous events in the USSR. Oddly enough, the newspaper reports, preserved by word-revering librarians on microfilm, survived longer. Television stations tended to re-use their videotape. It was only sheerest accident, and some on-site detective work by Gushie, that produced a single surviving video clip from the relevant period.

And for all its bragging, the computer was unable to obtain full access to sealed juvenile records.

So Ziggy split the big screen in Sam's office, showing the newspaper reports on one side and the TV announcer on the other, static report versus ninety-second view of the notions shop, stills of the victims, and the commentary by the bright-eyed brunette reporter.

That was all they had to work with.

That, and the hope that this report was in the wrong past.

"This can't be right," Al protested. "The first time you told me there was only one victim. I know you did! What the hell is going on?"

Unbidden, Ziggy froze on the photographs. Lily Sanchez's was taken at a family Christmas party, and she was laughing; she looked like a woman who laughed a great deal in her daily life. She was holding a daughter on her lap, a three-year-old who showed the mix of Asian and Hispanic blood to considerable advantage. This was a little girl who would grow up to be beautiful. This was a little girl who would grow up without her mother.

The second picture looked like a blowup of a candid snap, blurred and grainy.

"That wasn't there the first time," Al said desperately. "It wasn't there."

Ziggy hummed, still presenting the photograph of the second victim without comment. A serious-looking boy, with dark hair, looking past the camera at something behind the picture taker. The viewer couldn't tell what color his eyes were, but he had the mark of the black Irish in his expression and in his bones.

"Ziggy, do you remember this from the first time you accessed this history?"

"The first time I presented the data, we did not have this information." The computer blinked through the spectrum in rapid order. "I am unable to determine whether this report covers the same past as the one we originally reviewed."

"Ziggy, it *can't* be right. If this is right, then—"

"Then Ross Malachy is killed attempting to prevent the robbery. And since Dr. Beckett is currently residing in Mr. Malachy's body, presumably Dr. Beckett also dies.

"This will not, however, affect our current existence, since Dr. Beckett remains on his original life 'string.' I am more concerned with another report."

"*Another* report?"

"Yes." The lights rippled again. "I do not wish to present it, as I am uncertain of the reality in which it exists. However, I request that you make every effort to review your memories of this particular period of your life, so th-that we may. . . ." The computer was speaking in a more stilted manner than usual; now it actually stammered. Al wasn't familiar enough with Ziggy's internal workings to understand what that meant. "So that we may cross-reference as much information as possible."

Al didn't like the answer. He chewed ferociously at the end of his cigar. Ziggy, however, had the patience of one to whom milliseconds were virtually endless opportunities for self-checking anyway, and Al knew better than to think he could outwait the computer.

"What happens to Sam's body?" he said at last.

Ziggy's mechanical voice sounded surprised and displeased. "Are you planning to abandon Dr. Beckett?"

"I am *not*." Al was equally displeased. "I'm making contingency plans. Somebody has to think about Ross, who's trapped up there in Sam's body. We need to know what would happen to him if Sam dies. I know you've considered the possibility before. Spit it out."

"This particular visitor is young enough that he might be able to adjust," the computer mused. "The most likely scenario is that he would go mad. But adjustment is possible. It is to his advantage that he is of the same sex and approximate ethnic background as Dr. Beckett, as that simplifies a number of potential conflicts.

"Of course, it will be extraordinarily difficult to convince Dr. Beckett's friends and family, not to mention the Project's government sponsors, that Dr. Beckett has not simply gone insane. So even if Mr. Malachy can adjust to Dr. Beckett's body, it is doubtful that our world can adjust to him. The odds are very high that he will remain in treatment for the rest of the body's life."

"And?" Al pressed relentlessly.

"This scenario has, of course, been revisited and adjusted as data are accumulated. We have, therefore, set aside a place for Dr. Beckett—for Dr. Beckett's body to be safeguarded, no matter what the condition of the occupying entity, should he for any reason prove not able to return to the Project.

"In order to preclude questions, it will be necessary to report that he has died in an unavoidable accident. Off site, of course, since the kind of safety inspection triggered by an on-site accident is to be avoided. A one-vehicle accident is currently considered optimum. I will be able to manipulate reports to show that the body has been identified as Dr. Beckett's."

"And what happens to the body that *is* Dr. Beckett's?"

A long silence, punctuated by the rippling lights. "A place has been set aside."

"For how long?" Al whispered. "He's young yet."

"Dr. Beckett's body may last a long time," the computer agreed. "It's a strong body. Ross Malachy appears to have a strong mind. The predicted life span—"

"No." Al stood up, tossed the cigar into a nearby wastebasket. "No, that's enough." He turned and left the office without another word.

"I do sympathize, Admiral," the computer murmured, lights flickering.

In the military that Al Calavicci served in, seeing a psychiatrist was an excellent way of sabotaging one's hopes for promotion. The military had a see-no-evil attitude that saw seeking help for a problem as admitting one had a problem to begin with, and no one with problems ever commanded in this man's navy.

It was a stupid attitude. Al knew it was stupid; he'd known it was stupid when he dodged psychological assessment after being repatriated from Vietnam. He'd even acknowledged it was silly when dodging divorce counseling. Seeking help for a problem showed a healthy willingness to deal with reality. But he still didn't like the idea of psychiatry.

Verbeena Beeks, however, was the most soothing woman he had ever met. She was elegant and beautiful and wise and given to wearing brightly colored flowing caftans that gave her the look of sub-Saharan royalty. Sometimes they were temporarily subdued by a white lab coat, but for the most part Al found Verbeena's attire very simpatico.

Now he wanted more than simpatico clothing. He wanted someone to spill his guts to. Verbeena, who was responsible for the Visitors in the Waiting Room, was the logical choice.

In order to get to Verbeena, he had to go through the Waiting Room.

In the Waiting Room, where the body of Sam Beckett rested, and awoke, from time to time, with someone who was not Sam Beckett looking out of his eyes. Where people who were not Sam Beckett would get up, look down at the body they occupied, and scream. Every single time, they screamed.

Sam's throat was going to be awfully sore when he got back.

"Ziggy," he said as he stalked down the corridor, his right hand twitching for lack of a cigar, "ask Verbeena to meet me in the cafeteria, okay?"

Lisa loitered by the nurses' station, waiting for Ross to get back from wherever he'd gone, watching the nurses. One older one smiled at her, not really seeing her, shuffling through charts. The others were all too busy, running back and forth doing nurse things.

It might be interesting to be a nurse, Lisa thought. They did a lot of stuff. They got to use the needles and take pills and things in to the patients, and they could mess around with I.V.s and make notes on the charts.

But the doctors told them what to do. Except when there weren't any doctors around, which seemed like most of the time. Then there were the interns, who were almost like doctors but not quite.

Like this one with the chart, who came up to the nurse who smiled sometimes and said, "Who's doing that ovarian Tuesday?"

They talked about the patients that way. Not "that woman," or "that guy," or even "that person." It was all "that liver" or "that ovarian" or "that jelly roll in the corner." That was some really fat guy. Lisa traced a pattern on the counter from the circle of wetness left by someone's Coke can and listened.

The nurse shook her head. "We haven't got a release signed yet."

"Have you talked to the husband?"

"Yes, Doctor." She was letting her impatience show. That made it pretty sure this was an intern. "The husband says it's his wife's decision."

"Well, hell, how are we supposed to clean her out if we can't cut? Wasn't Zahmore scheduled for this? He's really going to be pissed—"

"It's the patient's decision, Doctor."

"The patient doesn't know what's good for her."

Lisa snorted softly. They sounded just like parents.

"Look at these tests." The intern was flipping through the chart. "That CA-125 is over 300. Shadows on the liver, spots all over the lung. We've got to get in there and clean her out, start chemo, radiation—I'm not sure that surgery would even do any good. This lady's terminal."

Lisa remained by the counter, staring down at her finger. Last night, when Ross had come to her room, he'd said her mother was going to die. He had said she had ovarian cancer.

She hadn't really believed him. What would Ross Malachy know? He was weird anyway. Her mother wasn't going to die. She tried to shut away the voices. This discussion had nothing to do with her, with her family. Ross was a liar. Liar. Liar. Her father wouldn't do that. He wouldn't leave her mother here alone to make a decision like that. He wouldn't. Wouldn't—

"We need to get the husband back in here to talk some sense to her. You should—"

"As I said, Doctor, you might try talking to the patient directly." The nurse sounded like she didn't want to sound like she was mad, but she really was. "The husband won't be coming in until later this evening. He said he had meetings to conduct, and this decision was his wife's. I don't see how hounding the man is going to change that."

"Okay." The intern got the message. "We'll just have to talk to the patient, then. Damn poor procedure, if you ask me." He flipped the chart shut, glared at the nurse, and walked down the hall, his heels clicking hard, telegraphing his irritation.

Lisa, eyes blank and throat dry, watched him go, denying his destination to herself. But as the intern proceeded, her denials crumbled; before he disappeared into her mother's room, she stepped away from the counter and walked in the opposite direction, toward the elevators.

Sam came back from radiology, looked around.

"Did you see a young girl around here?" he asked the charge nurse.

"Hmmm? Oh, yes, she was here a minute or two ago."

There had to be some way for him to signal Al, Sam thought, some way that he could let Al know that he needed the Observer's ability to home in on someone and report back on that location. It would make things so much easier. At first he thought she might have gone down the hall to use the bathroom, but when she didn't reappear in ten minutes he began to get anxious. He asked a wheelchair-equipped doctor who was heading that direction anyway to check it out for him, and was no longer surprised when minutes later she informed him, with regret, that no one else had used the facility while she was in it.

He stilled his first impulse to race down to the gift shop, to check the chapel, to look in on the cafeteria, and concentrated. As he did so he saw the intern come out of Jenniver Wales's room and march up to the nurses' station, tossing a chart onto the counter. A stray cup of coffee wobbled with the impact.

"She says she doesn't want surgery," he snapped. "This is crazy. What's it going to take to get that idiot to sign a release?"

The nurses glanced at each other and remained silent.

"Excuse me." Sam was beginning to get a dreadful suspicion. "Were you out here just a few minutes ago?"

"No," the intern said, facing him. "I use a transporter to get from one place to another. Yes, of course I was out here."

Sam took into account the lines on the other's face, the dark circles under his eyes. He remembered bits and pieces of his own time as an intern, and the all-pervading tiredness that characterized being on call seventy-two hours straight. He refrained from responding to the other man's tone in kind. "Did you see a teenage girl standing here when you discussed that patient?"

"How the hell should I know?"

The charge nurse spoke up. "Yes, she was standing right there. Haven't you found her yet?"

"I was concerned that she might have overheard your discussion about the patient in room 2316."

"I don't know if she did or not. Why? What does it matter?"

"I think she did," the nurse said. "I don't see how she couldn't have."

"So?" The intern was rubbing his eyes. "Go look in Lost and Found. I have patients to worry about."

"It matters," Sam informed him gently, "because that teenage girl is the daughter of the patient you were discussing. And if you were talking about her mother in the tone of voice *I* overheard you using, she's probably in a state of shock right now. So you probably have one more patient to worry about than you thought." He left doctor and nurse staring at each other in consternation.

The window in the waiting room overlooked the parking lot; he headed for it, hoping that he'd find the truck still parked in the shade of the giant cottonwood.

There was no truck. It had been replaced by someone's new minivan. Sam closed his eyes and swore, very softly. Swearing was something he reserved for very special occasions. This was one of them.

Without wheels, he was stuck, at least temporarily. He seemed to recall that there was bus service on a fairly regular basis all up and down the main city arteries. A quick check with a rather subdued charge nurse produced the relevant schedule; the next bus wasn't due for another half hour.

It gave him time to look in on Jenniver and see how much damage the abrasive intern had done. He wasn't surprised to find her wiping away the traces of tears. She was startled to see him again, pulling the thin hospital sheet and blanket up protectively over the quilted bed jacket that Lisa, of all of them, had remembered to bring for her to wear.

"Ross? Is something wrong?"

Sam winced mentally. "Just checking one more time to see how you're doing. Lisa's already at the car. I guess the doctor came in to talk to you."

It almost started her crying again, but she clamped down on her emotions and became very regal in her effort to control herself. "Yes, he did."

"Mrs. Wales, I know you said this was none of my business, and you're right, in a way." *And you're wrong, too, because Something has* made *this kind of thing my business whether I want it to be or not!* "But I know what the doctor wants, and if you're going to have any chance, any chance at all, you have to have the surgery. Please, Mrs. Wales. Lisa needs you, more than you even know.

"You should do this for yourself, and you should do it for your family. Please."

She wasn't looking at him; she was looking instead at the cheerful little cluster of white-and-yellow daisies that he and Lisa had stopped off in the gift shop to buy. He had given them to Lisa to carry while he had hauled along the overnight case. Lisa had held them out to her mother without a word, a silent offering. Jenniver had never taken her eyes off them for the whole visit.

"We can't afford it," she said, so quietly he had to strain to hear. "All these tests. The ambulance. They charge you a dollar and a half for every aspirin, did you know that? Surgery is expensive too. You pay for the surgeon, and the anesthesiologist, and the operating room.

"My aunt Sylvia got sick this way, and her family never did pay it off. Thousands and thousands of dollars. And now they have all the new treatments, new 'protocols' that doctor was telling me. All the different things they can try. And I'm going to die anyway, just like Sylvia."

She looked at Sam then, dry-eyed. "My daughter needs money for college, and we can barely pay the bills as it is. Can you tell me why we should spend that money on operations for me if all I'm going to do is die anyway?"

CHAPTER

TWENTY

The Project cafeteria consisted of a small dining area with cheap tables and chairs, and a kitchen with three microwave/convection ovens and a large, glass-doored freezer stocked with frozen dinners. The shelves on the opposite wall were stocked with cans of soup and vegetables. Beside the sink, an industrial coffeepot bubbled. The windows were draped in cream-colored curtains left over from one of Tina's decorating frenzies; their delicate lace contrasted oddly with the gray linoleum of the floor.

Al had just gotten a pair of mugs from one of the cabinets and was searching for milk when Verbeena came in. She was wearing her lab coat, and carrying with her a familiar chart.

"How's our latest Visitor doing?" Al said. He found the milk and poured out a mug. Verbeena took her coffee white. Al, a purist, added nothing at all. It didn't matter. Nothing could improve the taste of Project coffee.

They sat at one of the tables, sipped, and grimaced in unison. The work of the Project meant that people dropped in at all hours of the day and night; it was dinnertime, which generally meant the place was deserted. Al had counted on that quirk in Project psychology.

"Well," Verbeena said, "not too badly, considering. He thinks he's been kidnapped by aliens."

"That's nothing new."

Verbeena smiled. She was a willowy black woman who could have been anywhere from 30 to 50. When she signed up to work for Sam Beckett, she never expected the kind of psychiatric practice she found here, treating the shocked and terrified people who found themselves trapped in the body of a scientist years in their future. It had taken her a while to adjust to the idea that each time she saw a new patient, it would be in the same old body. She quickly learned to deal with it in the same quiet, efficient, caring manner that she cared for everyone else on the Project, whether they were under treatment or not.

"What is it this time, Al? It's not Ross Malachy. Who's really pretty much okay, all things considered."

Al took a deep breath. "What would you say if I told you that we don't exist?"

"I would say that you're getting existential."

"It's true. At least, as far as Ziggy can tell, it's true. Sam's remembering that I said things I can't remember saying, we can't nail down what really happened in the robbery, and it's possible that Ross gets killed. At least it looks that way now."

The psychiatrist pursed her lips. "Mondo bummer, Admiral."

Al gave her an exasperated look. "Your age is showing. Besides, I'm serious."

She shook her head. "I saw the initial history; the only person who was killed was the woman in the store. Oh, and the mother, but that was a natural death that didn't even happen for some time."

"And now Ziggy has newspaper reports that show Ross getting shot trying to prevent the robbery. Which really means Sam. I don't know what to tell Sam, Verbeena." He turned the mug around and around in his hands, the gold silhouette of a Stealth fighter on a black mug rotating under his fingers. "I don't know which past he's in, if it's the one where he saves the kid, in which case he's gotta do it so he can Leap, or if it's the one where he could get killed. Ziggy doesn't even want to offer odds any more."

"And seeing yourself in the past is unnerving you too."

"Yeah, it is." He took a deep swallow. "It bothers me a lot."

"Why?" Verbeena probed gently. "What happened back then that upsets you so much?"

Al shrugged, refusing to meet her eyes. "It was just a really bad time for me, that's all. All kinds of changes happening at once. I came so close to taking this other job, a consultant gig—" He set the mug down, precisely in the circular mark left by some coffee spill from the past. "I'm scared that something is going to talk me into taking it. And if that happens, what will happen to me in the here and now?"

He took a deep breath and continued. "What's going on here, what really bothers me, is that if you follow Sam's theory that your life is like a string, then we've got to realize that his string is a lot longer than any of ours. Our lives are all straight lines, the shortest way between two points, from when we're born to right this second.

"But Sam's been looping back and forth all over the place. Still one string, but all wadded up."

"I'm not sure I understand what's troubling you, Al," Verbeena said. She had the nonjudgmental air of the therapist down pat, he noticed.

"Don't you see? When Sam is right now, his string is crossing mine, and it isn't supposed to. I'm not looping around the way he is; in 1990, that was all I had. Now he's gone back and he's changing things, and maybe he'll change things for me, too."

"Well, if you're still here, I'd say he probably didn't succeed."

"But what if he does, in this different past that we seem to be in?"

"What do you remember about the incident? Can you recall who died?"

Al poked the mug out of alignment. "Ah. No."

In a small, startled silence, Verbeena leaned forward. "Al?"

"I'm sorry," he exploded, jumping to his feet and pacing back and forth, arms flailing. "On the one hand everything was turning to shit in my life, and this encounter stuff was just one more crazy thing I was doing. I didn't want to remember it. I thought it was damned silly. On the other hand"— he spun around theatrically—"I was really trying to get something out of it, you know? And then

216

I had to get back to Washington, and Sam was there. And Sam's the one with the photographic memory. I'm just a normal human being. And I just don't remember! It was ten years ago, dammit!"

Sam opened his mouth and then closed it again. He couldn't offer false reassurances. He'd told Lisa what Ziggy had said, what the future held, and he couldn't lie to her mother now.

"Everybody dies eventually," he got out finally. "Isn't life worth fighting for?"

"Have you ever seen anyone die this way?" Jenniver asked in response. Without waiting for an answer, she went on, "Your hair falls out, you know, and you can't eat because of the nausea. Your teeth get so loose in your gums, and they bleed. Your gums, that is. And your skin gets so thin, so sensitive, you feel like anything that touches you hurts. A feather could touch you, and you scream." She was talking from memory now, looking once again at the white-and-yellow flowers. "I used to change the bed sheets for Sylvia. She didn't have control of her bowels, you see. She would be so ashamed. And all I could do was pretend that nothing was the matter, that everything was okay.

"My father left all that to me, you see. My mother had died when I was five, and he couldn't face going through it again. Aunt Sylvia was only thirty-six when she got sick. And I was twelve, taking care of her."

"And Lisa's only fifteen. Are you going to ask her to do things for you the way you had to for Sylvia?"

"I'm not going to ask her to do anything for me. I wouldn't ask her to do that."

He closed his eyes, reviewing the anger of the last few days. "Maybe you ought to."

She shook her head. "I couldn't."

He wanted to argue with her, do whatever it took to convince her, but time was running out. He didn't want to leave so abruptly, but he had no choice. "I'm sorry. I've got to catch a bus. I wish—"

She glanced at him inquiringly, and he shook his head. "I guess everybody really is right. It's up to you. You're the only one who can decide."

He made the bus just in time, and stood swaying, scrambling in his pocket for the correct change, hoping that Lisa had taken the Blazer home to confront her father. He didn't know where else to go. He nodded at the student sitting with his legs stretched out in the aisle, stepped over the legs, and kept an eye on the passing streets. It was a modern bus with a handicap lift, and it stopped twice to accept passengers in wheelchairs. He studied the mechanism, unable to remember if he had ever seen it actually in use before.

The bus dropped him off a half-dozen blocks away from the house. He checked his watch again. It was three o'clock.

He jogged to the house, wondering what he was going to do if Lisa wasn't there.

And she wasn't. Wales came out of his study as he walked in the front door.

"Oh, Ross, I'm glad you're here. We need to think about getting ready to go to the hotel—"

"Have you seen Lisa?" Sam interrupted him.

"No, of course not. She went to the hospital with you. You didn't leave her there, did you?"

"She left *me* there," Sam said bitterly. "I'll bet she's got the weapon now, too."

"Weapon? What are you talking about?" Stephen Wales peered at him through the heavy lenses, his eyes magnified and wild. "What would Lisa want with something like that?"

"Lisa got one of your guns and gave it to her friend Stenno," Sam explained.

"Oh no, that's silly. All the guns are locked in the cabinet in my office."

"All but one. Where would Lisa go—"

"Oh no, she couldn't get into my gun cabinet. It's locked." He led Sam back into the study, scrabbled in his desk. "See? There's the key."

"Look in the cabinet," Sam said through gritted teeth.

"It's nonsense, I tell you. But if that's the only thing that will satisfy you—" He pushed past and jiggled the lock open, swinging the cabinet doors wide to reveal an old .30–.30 and a double-barreled shotgun. Sam breathed a sigh of relief at the sight of the shotgun. At least Lisa didn't "borrow" that one to pass along to her boyfriend.

"Oh my god," Wales said.

"What?"

Wales turned, and Sam stepped back at the sight of the automatic in his hand.

"It's gone," the older man said, unaware that the line of fire of the gun he was holding was wavering across Ross Malachy's torso. "The other gun is gone."

Sam stepped rapidly to one side and in to grasp Stephen's wrist and take the automatic away from him. As he did so he caught sight of a cleaning kit and several boxes of ammunition lying on the floor of the cabinet, hidden by the lower lip. "What other gun?"

"The revolver. The .38. It was my first gun, my father gave it to me. And it's gone."

"At least she didn't take the bullets," Sam said, replacing the automatic.

"Oh, it was loaded." Wales was speaking absently, feeling around in the base of the cabinet as if the gun must still be there, it was only invisible somehow. "A gun isn't much use without any bullets in it."

"You leave *loaded guns* lying around in this house?"

"Well, the cabinet's locked. No one's supposed to get into it. Are you sure Lisa took it? Why would she do that? She's never been interested in weapons before. When she was eight, I took her out to the pistol range. I thought if I was going to have guns in the house, I should make sure everyone knew how to use them safely. But all she did was cry and put her hands over her ears. She wouldn't even try. I can't imagine that she'd take one."

Sam closed his eyes and took a deep breath, considering and rejecting a dozen responses. "Lisa took the gun. Lisa took the truck."

"She doesn't have a driver's license," her father objected.

"Believe it or not, Dr. Wales," Sam bit off each word individually, "teenagers can and do drive before they get their licenses. She took the car. Trust me. Now, where would she go?"

The other man stared at him, biting hard on his lower lip. "Why would my daughter take a gun? What's she going to do with it?"

He had already told the man that she was going to give it to Stenno. It dawned on him, as he watched Wales struggle to maintain his composure, that he'd also already answered his own question.

"Where does Stenno live?" he asked.

"I—I don't know." At the look in Sam's eyes, he added hastily, "I think her teachers know. I could call them."

"Why don't you do that. We're going to have to catch them before the mall closes."

Fortunately or otherwise, Wales didn't ask what the mall had to do with anything.

"My group," Wales protested feebly.

"Look," Sam said, patience gone at last. "You're going to have to make up your mind what's most important to you. Is it this damned group of yours, or is it your wife and daughter? Your wife is sitting in the hospital afraid to get the surgery that might save her life, and your daughter is about to get herself in more trouble than any kid can possibly cope with, and you're still talking about your damned encounter group!"

"But those men need me."

"Your family needs you!"

"I'm doing this for my family!" Wales shouted back at him. "How do you think I can afford to pay for those doctor bills? I have to have this meeting!" Tears threatened to spill from his eyes, absurdly magnified behind the heavy lenses. The professor's voice and body were both shaking. Wales was about as far from being the confident, assured encounter group leader of the day before as he was from Mars.

With a gut-wrenching twist of empathy, Sam realized that it was as if someone else, someone uncertain and frightened and wholly unable to cope with the escalating demands on his time and emotional resources had Leaped into Wales's body, sending the competent, withdrawn, emotionally isolated person he once was somewhere else to occupy someone else's body. Stephen Wales was on the thin edge of a breakdown. Sam backed off, physically as well as psychically, unwilling to put any more pressure on him.

"Dr. Wales," he said, "with the scale of bills you're looking at—and believe me, I know how bad they can be—the fees from one more meeting can't make that much difference. The important thing now is *time*. You can't afford to delay Jenniver's surgery; you can't afford to ignore what's going on with Lisa."

"I can't talk to Lisa," Wales whispered. "She never listens to me. You know how she is. You've seen."

"And you don't listen to her, either. You need to apply some of your own principles to her. You can't abdicate being a father because it doesn't work very well." He sneaked a look at his watch. It was nearly four o'clock. "Look, if you'll find out where Stenno lives, I can check that out. You take a cab to the hospital and talk to your wife. I'll deal with Lisa this time."

"Will you?" The man was almost pathetically grateful, clinging to the door of the cabinet as if it were the only thing keeping him on his feet. Color was beginning to return to his face along with hope. "Jenniver's keys—" He held them out to Sam as if they were a peace offering. "You could take the sedan."

"*This* time," Sam reiterated firmly, hoping it was true and taking the keys anyway. "Next time it's going to be strictly up to you. She's your daughter. Maybe you ought to go into counseling together."

"And maybe there won't be time," Al said from behind him, his voice uncharacteristically grim. "You'd better get over there fast if you're going to catch them, Sam."

Sam had long since learned to cover his start of surprise when Al popped in on him. He wasn't always completely successful, however. Nonetheless, he recovered smoothly this time and said, "Come to think of it, I think I can figure out where Stenno lives—"

"7216 Kathleen NE," Al supplied without missing a beat.

"—so you call a cab and get down to the hospital." Seeing the man waver again, he added, "Call the hotel too and tell them there's been a family emergency, and you've had to postpone the meeting. You'll get back to them as soon as possible. Have them put up a sign"— *that ought to make Ms. Clearwater happy*— "so the participants will know what's happened."

He didn't wait to see if Wales agreed; he didn't even wait to see if the other man let go of the cabinet door. Al jabbed at the handlink, yelling at Gushie to keep the Observer centered on Sam, as Sam disappeared out the door, heading for the car and for Lisa.

CHAPTER
TWENTY-ONE

Stenno Baczek stood in front of a mirror, trying to twirl the revolver the way they did in his favorite cowboy movies. He hardly ever talked about them, but he would rather stay up late with *The Magnificent Seven* or an old John Wayne flick than MTV. They just didn't show old westerns much any more.

He narrowed his eyes and peered up into a corner like Gary Cooper checking out the roofs as he walked down Main Street in *High Noon,* holding the gun at his side. He really wanted a holster, so he could practice a quick draw, but he would take what he could get. He wanted a wisp of hay to stick in the corner of his mouth, too, but he had never seen real hay, so a toothpick had to do. He rolled it back and forth from one side to the other and looked for the bad guys in the mirror.

It wasn't as if he'd never handled a gun before. He had, lots of times, but the guns he had admired in school were usually automatics, brought in by other students trying to impress their peers. And there weren't so very many of them, either; Stenno's school, the one he attended before he decided there were more interesting things to do with his time, was far from being hard-core. His brother-in-law's auto-repair shop provided him with work when he felt like working, and the daylight robberies inspired by looking over auto registrations and copying house keys left on the car-key ring provided enough to support his apartment and some drugs. He'd never needed a gun before.

But this one—this was cool. This was Wayne and Cooper and Eastwood.

He spun the gun again, awkwardly, and the trigger caught on his finger and slid off, the weapon landing with a thud, barrel facing toward him. It took a moment to realize that the weapon hadn't fired, and he started breathing again, unable to restrain the nervous grin on his face.

He'd have to find a way to carry it under his jacket without being too conspicuous. He was considering ways to rig a shoulder holster when someone started beating on the apartment door and ringing the bell over and over again.

Spinning around, he started toward the door, gun in hand. The other hand was on the doorknob as he peered through the peephole. The bell rang again, shrill and impatient. Swearing, he ran over to the couch and stuffed the gun underneath a cushion.

Lisa had lifted her hand to strike the door again as he opened it. She nearly fell into his arms. She was crying hysterically.

He had no choice but to catch her; there wasn't enough room to let her collapse. She clung to him for the space of perhaps three sobs before he was able to take her by the shoulders and push her away.

"What the hell is the matter with you?" He still had hold of her shoulders. Without the support, she would have fallen forward again. The tone of his voice was the only thing to reach her. She looked up at him and burst into a fresh spate of tears.

"Stop it!" he yelled, shaking her. "Stop it!"

There was no place in this apartment that she could let go of her emotions. The realization came to her with the impact of her head against the door as it flopped back with the jerking of his hands on her. With a gasp, she stopped crying.

He let go, and she dashed the tears from her face, sniffing. Her face was blotched and puffy, her hair hanging in strings.

"You look like shit," he informed her, stepping back and letting her into the living room. "What happened?"

"I was at the hospital with Ross," she said at last. "I heard them talking. My mom's going to die because my dad won't sign some papers so she can have an operation. He's killing her."

"Wow." Temporarily speechless, more from a lack of the ability to empathize than from shock, Stenno closed the door behind her. "That's, like, murder."

She nodded, fiercely. "Right. It's murder." She looked around for a tissue to blow her nose. The apartment was cluttered with hamburger wrappers and paper sacks and a couple of comic books. The plaid couch in the corner, held up by a pair of cinder blocks on one end, sagged in the middle. Little tufts of dried-out rubber foam stuck out along the seams, souvenirs of some long-ago cat's claw exercise. The living room opened out into a small kitchen; another door led into a bedroom. With the sureness of long familiarity Lisa walked through the bedroom and into the bathroom beyond, coming out again with a fistful of yellow toilet paper. She blew her nose and swallowed and looked up at Stenno again.

"I don't want to go back there," she said. "I don't ever want to see him again. I hate him."

"That's cool." He flopped down on the couch, intensely aware of the gun underneath the pillow. Lisa didn't know about his going to get the gun; she thought it was still where she'd dropped it, underneath the lilac bush outside the bathroom window. It was exciting to know the gun was there, to know that she was the means of his having it, and that she didn't know.

She was, he thought with deep satisfaction, not only ugly with the marks of her weeping, but stupid too.

"You want to stay with me?" Not that he wanted to have her around all the time; she was fun sometimes, but the rest of the time Lisa was a pain in the ass, always hanging on him, always wanting to be reassured about how he felt and how much he needed her.

She took a deep shuddering breath and nodded.

Hell, he could pick up a dozen like her on East Central any night of the week. But for the time being it was convenient. He glanced at the clock in the kitchen, subtracted ten minutes because it always ran fast. Four o'clock.

"Hey, baby." He got up then and went over to her, nuzzling. Statutory rape, they called this. He didn't see how it could be rape when she wanted it as much as he did. But this time she pulled away. "Hey. You don't have to stay there if you don't want to. You're my woman, my strong woman, right?" He embraced her again, but loosely, so that she wouldn't have an excuse to fight it.

She assented, both to the words and the embrace, but she was looking away. "I hate him."

"Hey, that's cool. I don't get along with my old man so hot, either. But I'm really glad you came, you know? I was afraid you'd forget."

She looked up at him, startled, and he realized that she really had forgotten.

"You know? We were going over to the mall, hang out some, see if we could get some excitement, right?" He breathed deep into her hair.

She stepped out of the circle of his arms. "I don't want to go to the mall," she said scornfully. "That's like some kids or something. 'Let's go to the mall.' How juvenile." The color on her face was evening out again, the swelling from her tears was going down. She was looking better and better.

His lips tightened and his nostrils flared, responding to her scorn. "Hey!"

"Well, it is! That's what all the kids would do. I want to do something else. Something grown up."

He moved forward involuntarily. "I know something grown up we could do. . . ."

Casting a glance sideways at him, she snorted. "Yeah, I bet. That's not what I mean. I want to do something *important*."

With difficulty, he refocused himself. He had plans. Other things could happen later. "I didn't want to just hang out," he said. "Remember the scarf?"

"What about the scarf?" she said slowly.

"I was thinking about something along those lines. We could get something really nice. Something you could give your mom in the hospital," he improvised, pulling her in. She lifted a hand to rub the place where her head had hit the door. "You don't need your dad to get stuff," he added. "You can do it yourself. You're my strong woman. You don't need anybody. You can take care of yourself and your mom too. Right?"

It would take some coaxing, he saw, to bring her to the point he wanted her to reach. Lisa was still too much the good girl. But once they were in the store, once he had the gun out, she wouldn't have any choice. She'd have to play along.

If she didn't, of course, he could always kill her, too. He narrowed his eyes to look over her head at the vision of a western street. Yup. That would do it.

The difference between Gary Cooper's role and the part he planned to play never even occurred to him. They both carried guns, after all. That was enough.

Well, there was one more thing: They both could kill.

Al was following the twists and turns of pieces of a city map as transmitted by Ziggy through the handlink, trying to guide Sam to the apartment.

"Where have you *been*?" Sam asked through gritted teeth. "There hasn't been any rhyme nor reason for the way you've been showing up and disappearing on this Leap, and you haven't been explaining things too well, either. I wish you'd tell me what the matter was."

Al closed his eyes. Even after his talk with Verbeena, he still didn't know what to do. Ziggy was no help either. If he told Sam that in the process of stopping the robbery, there was a high probability he'd be killed, Sam would take a deep breath and charge in anyway, willing to take his chances in order to save Lisa's future. On the other hand, if Sam did nothing, he—in Ross Malachy's body—would live; but the probability was almost 100 percent that the innocent shop owner would die and Lisa's life would be destroyed. And Sam would be stuck in Ross Malachy's body, with Malachy stuck in Sam's, forever.

And if he explained the dilemma to Sam, all he'd get would be a look of total incomprehension. Sam was constitutionally incapable of doing nothing. He would place his trust in Whatever was causing him to Leap, completely disregarding the possibility that he might be expendable.

"I'm not dumb, I'm not expendable, and I'm not going," Al muttered under his breath. Al's whole life had molded his view of life in pragmatic terms. Survival came first, always. Then you took care of your buddies. You fought fair as long as you could, and then you did what had to be done.

Sam, on the other hand, was an altruist at heart. He might protest from time to time that the process of Leaping served everyone in the universe but Sam Beckett, but that would never stop him from doing what he considered the right thing.

And that, Al concluded, was why Sam Leaped and Al Observed. Somebody had to keep an eye on the kid. This white-knight business could be dangerous.

It was a comforting paradigm, even if it wasn't totally correct.

"You're not answering me," Sam pointed out. They were still a mile away from Stenno's address, stopped at a red light. The driver of the car behind them was getting impatient; it looked like the light was stuck.

"I have to check something," Al said. He jabbed at the controls.

"Wait a minute, you can't leave now!"

"Gotta," Al said, and stepped back through the Door.

Verbeena Beeks was waiting for him, a silent statue of support. Beside her, standing around the control table, Tina looked scared and gorgeous. Next to her, holding her hand, was Gushie, whose anxious expression could have meant something or nothing at all.

"I'm going to have to do it," Al said. "I don't know any other way."

"This isn't in any of the histories at all," Gushie said. "You'll be throwing a real money wrench into things." He let go of Tina's hand as soon as he realized Al had noticed and hid his own hands behind his back, like an oversized child caught filching cookies. "We can't predict what might happen."

"There is a worst-case scenario." Ziggy's voice emanated from the ceiling. "There is a possibility that the entire Project will be irreversibly changed."

"That's possible anyway," Al said. "Look, we haven't got much time. Gushie, Ziggy—center me on me."

CHAPTER

TWENTY-TWO

Al Calavicci glanced around the hotel room. The week of work at the Labs had just been canceled. He had one more meeting at the Labs tomorrow morning, a quick lunch with the program director, and then he'd be catching a flight back to Washington. Packing was never much of a problem when all you carried was a small, battered brown suitcase and a garment bag. When you were in the military, you learned to travel light and carry only those things that were really important. He didn't really have to pack yet; pulling everything together would take five minutes in the morning. He'd dump the bag in the trunk of the rental car, and after lunch head directly for the airport. Straightforward. Efficient. No nonsense about it.

And then spend five hours—counting the damned layover in Dallas, but it was either Dallas or St. Louis, and he'd pick Dallas almost anytime, except

January—on the plane, going back to divorce hearings and final briefings and decisions about the rest of his life, with nothing at all to do but think about things. Think about life after retirement, and what the hell he was going to do with himself.

He hadn't realized it until he got the call from the front desk, but he'd actually been looking forward to that last encounter group meeting. It would have taken up some time on a late Sunday afternoon. Time was weighing heavy these days with no immediate goals, no projects, no camaraderie. Life after retirement was starting to look like a bleak, endless road through the unknown.

Punctuated from time to time by leggy blondes, he reminded himself. Redheads. The occasional brunette. Once he was out of uniform, he could indulge himself—discreetly, of course, Al Calavicci was always a gentleman, if a randy one. And he wouldn't even be married. He'd have no strings at all to tie him down. He'd be footloose, fancy free, voting age and fully equipped. Okay, so even an Admiral's retirement pay was nothing to shout about, but there was that job offer, too. There were still a few pleasures out there to be sampled.

Like cigars.

Damn, that was what he meant to do—pick up more cigars. The Labs were persnickety about smoking, but he just didn't feel dressed when he was out of uniform and didn't have a cigar in his hand. He checked his watch. If he hurried, he could get to that little smoke shop in the mall before they closed. He reached for his car keys.

At the door to his hotel room he paused. He was forgetting something, he was sure of it. His gaze scanned the surfaces in the room, losing focus as they crossed the little table by the window and sharpening again. No, everything was there.

He looked at his watch again, seized with a sudden anxiety. He had to get to that smoke shop. He had to leave, right now.

The door closed behind him with a force that sent the molecules of dust dancing in the rays of sunlight coming through the venetian blinds. It was several minutes before they settled again, on the chairs, the bed, the table, the newly opened box of cigars.

Normally Al couldn't influence anything in Sam's "moment" of time. Animals and very small children could see him; Sam could see him; but that was all. He couldn't move anything, couldn't talk to anyone. He could go through barriers that would be solid walls to Sam as if they weren't even there; they weren't, really. The real Al was in the Imaging Chamber, deep in a fully dimensional hallucination created by Ziggy through the link that bound the three of them together. Ziggy could pick up information, somehow, that widened his scope beyond Sam's immediate vicinity; that was part of the physics that only Sam could understand. Al didn't pretend to.

He only knew that right now, he desperately needed to influence someone back in Sam's time, and so far, miraculously, it seemed to be working.

Of course, it made sense, in a weird way. He was the same Al, just in two different times. He tried at first to be "inside" himself, hoping that he'd be able to take over and give himself a reality beyond the virtual, but that didn't work. There seemed to be space for only one of him at a time in his 1990 body.

But he could exert a subtle influence somehow. He could shout in his own ear—funny, he'd never noticed that little brown mark on the upper ridge of his ear; he wondered abstractedly how long he'd had that, and if he still did—about the tobacconist's, which was next door to the notions shop. He could hold his "hands" over "his" eyes, in an effort to prevent himself from seeing a brand-new box of smokes sitting in plain sight on the table. It worked; at least, the 1990 Al was looking at his watch a lot, and the box was invisible, judging from the expression on his face. But he couldn't exactly tell what was going through his mind, and he couldn't recall any of this stuff ever happening. How important could it be, after all—going out to get a box of cigars?

He didn't like it at all, this business of floating around himself. He kept looking down at himself, checking to see if the natty subdued silver shirt with the matching dove-gray tie, brocaded in gold thread, and the elegant fog-gray suit were still there. He wished he'd picked something else out of the closet this morning. The outfit made him feel like a ghost, haunting himself.

The other Al, dressed in the same old boring khaki slacks and dark green polo shirt was driving hell-for-leather, skidding around cars and through yellow lights. Al-the-Observer was "riding" shotgun with him, yelling warnings, closing his eyes against crashes that looked impossible to avoid. "I didn't know I was such a good driver," he said to himself. Looking over at the man behind the wheel, he caught the last wisp of a self-satisfied grin, and shuddered, wondering if he'd heard himself.

In an odd way he was building a psychological distance. This was himself, the self of ten years previous, but it wasn't the person he was now. A lot of water had gone under the bridge since then, a lot of changes had occurred. It wasn't really him. Not the Al who worked on Quantum Leap. That was probably why he couldn't just tell himself what to do; this was a different man. He'd had different worries, different priorities.

Al-the-Observer had the advantage of having only one priority right now.

"Gushie, bounce me, okay? I want to check on Sam and Lisa."

The link was strongest to Sam, of course, so he went there first. Sam's driving was more conservative than Al's—which figured—so he was stopped at a red light, alternately drumming his fingers on and clenching the steering wheel, white-knuckled. He jumped when Al popped in beside him.

"For crying out loud, Sam, there isn't another car around for at least two blocks! Run the light!"

Sam shot him an exasperated glare. Just then the light changed, and he jackrabbited through, jolting himself back against the seat. Al, who wasn't subject to those particular laws of physics in this particular situation, shook his head.

"Quit criticizing and find out where Lisa is," Sam said through clenched teeth.

Al, his hand already poised over the handlink, shot him an injured look. "I *was* going to."

"Then *do* it!"

The scene in the Imaging Chamber blurred and jumped. Al had always been grateful, back when he was a jet jock and when he was in the space program, that he had a superb sense of equilibrium; it had served him well in tests of acceleration and weightlessness, allowing him to tolerate high gravities and stress. The folks at Lovelace Clinic, where they'd done astronaut testing, had never imagined he'd have to be able to keep his cookies in situations like this one.

It didn't help that he expected to be in an apartment complex, and instead found a pair of three-year-old African-American twins, dressed identically in cowboy suits topped with little, bright red buckaroo hats, playing tag right through his legs.

"Wha—?"

The boys, nearly as startled as he was, stopped, looked up, and put mirror-image thumbs in their mouths.

"Don't suck your thumbs," he said automatically.

Brown eyes narrowed, and identical "you're-not-the-boss-of-me" expressions crept across their faces.

Al gave up and looked around. This was no apartment complex—this was the mall. And there, at the far end of the garden court, just coming in through the glass doors, were Lisa and Stenno.

"Oh, no," Al muttered, looking at his watch. There was still a little—a very little—time.

"Gushie," he said, his voice strained. "Put me on Sam! Now!"

The twins had pulled toy six-guns from toy holsters, and were aiming carefully. Just as they said "Bang!", Al disappeared.

The two of them looked at the toy guns, looked at each other, giggled, and went looking for their big sister.

• • •

"Sam, you've got to turn around! They're already at the mall!"

The nose of the sedan was already in an intersection when Al reappeared. Without hesitation and without slowing down, Sam veered right to give himself the widest radius possible and dragged the steering wheel around to the left, rocking violently and barely missing a white Toyota coming from what had originally been the other direction. The Toyota's driver, an overweight woman with short brown hair, stood on the brakes and screamed an obscenity. Sam didn't even notice.

"Are they in the store yet?" he said, giving the car more gas.

"No, not yet."

"Then go and keep an eye on things. You can't help me here." Sam's voice was clipped, quiet. He gave his complete attention to driving. Al didn't think he even noticed when the hologram vanished.

Lisa and Stenno were only about twenty feet farther into the garden court when Al returned. Lisa was looking around uncertainly. The mall was within a half hour of closing, and only a few people were left, some hefting packages out to their cars, some strolling along quietly, enjoying ice-cream cones or giant pretzels. Perhaps a half dozen tables in the court were still occupied by shoppers who had stopped for a fast-food dinner.

Stenno was moving his head back and forth, checking things out. His eyes were very bright, and he carried his head high. He was breathing hard, almost panting with excitement, and his fair complexion was suffused with blood along the cheekbones as if he had developed a sudden, high fever. He had one hand on Lisa's arm as if to guide her, but he was standing almost still.

Al had once seen, at a county fair, a young stallion excited by the presence of mares in heat and other stallions to challenge. The horse had pranced and rolled his eyes and practically stood on tiptoe in his eagerness to engage in sex and battle.

Stenno looked like that now. His free hand kept ducking under his jacket, as if checking the presence, or perhaps the reality, of something there. Lisa asked him something, and he guided her over to a table and forced her down without answering. He went over to a nearby stand and got a couple of paper cups of lemonade, bringing it back to her and slapping it down hard enough that the drink slopped over onto Lisa's jeans.

The twins raced over and began circling, waving their toy guns. Al winced and started over, planning to shoo them far away, but the boys' mother got their first. Stenno was staring at the little six-guns, and a wolfish grin was spreading across his face.

"Jase! Josh! What have I told you about those guns! You give them here right this minute!"

Jase and Josh laughed and raced away. They caught sight of Al and stopped in their tracks.

"You listen to your mom," he said sternly.

The boys giggled and came closer. One gun passed through Al's right leg. Josh, who had planned to accidentally-on-purpose hit this strange white guy, stopped short, glancing at his brother for support.

Jase slowly moved his gun through Al's other leg. The two of them looked up at him, their mouths forming small o's of surprise.

"I hate to do this, but . . . I'm a ghost! And I'm telling you to go over to your mom and stay with her right now! *Boo!*" Raising his arms over his head and waving them around wildly, Al stamped his hologrammatic feet. The boys laughed, a soprano carillon. This ghost was the most fun they'd had all day.

Far down the mall, the sound of rattling metal announced that some store owner had decided to call it quits early.

It finally dawned on Al that the kids were interested in him, not in Stenno. He glanced back over his shoulder and almost choked as he saw Stenno rising to his feet. Al scurried through the twins. "Okay! You guys wanna play chase? You can't catch me!"

The little boys crowed with delight and spun around in hot pursuit, leaving Stenno flat-footed behind them. Al ducked and dodged around planters full of philodendrons, while the twins, strategists in the making, split up to cut him off at the pass.

It would have worked, except that Al cut completely through the planter; when his pursuers tried to emulate him they ended up stubbing toes against the tiled edging. They were still deciding whether this was something worth crying about when their mother descended like an avenging angel and swept them up, one under each arm. From the looks on the faces of mother and sons, this wasn't a particularly unusual occurrence. The boys cast pleading looks at their "ghost" to save them. Al shrugged, palms upward, and sighed with relief to see the three heading for the mall exit.

Stenno, balked, looked around. More chain doors were descending, stopping halfway in tacit acknowledgment that it was still early, that a stray customer might still make a last-minute purchase.

It was time.

Stenno checked under his jacket again, pulled at Lisa's arm. Al jabbed at the handlink. "Gushie! Where the hell is Sam!"

CHAPTER

TWENTY-THREE

Al Calavicci, Admiral, couldn't quite recall where the tobacconist's shop was. Somewhere down in the south wing of the mall, he thought, close to the west-side entrance. An irritated mother passed him on his way in; she was herding three children, a pair of obstreperous twins and a slightly older girl with her hair in tight cornrows. The twins were pointing at him with great excitement. He held the door for their mother and grinned at her rolled eyes and silent plea for understanding.

The directory was just inside, beside the escalator. He paused long enough to scan it, checking his location against the numbered blue and yellow squares.

Yeah, there it was. Halfway up. By the other entrance, around that bend. If he'd only parked on the other side of the mall he could have saved himself the walk. As it was, they were close to shutting down;

he glanced at his watch and picked up his pace. One good thing about the Navy, you learned when to cut in the afterburners.

He came around the corner. There was the tobacconist, right next to that little sewing shop. The tobacconist was puttering around, showing all the signs of getting ready to close down for the evening. The lady in the sewing shop still had a couple of customers, a teenage girl, and a punk of a boyfriend who was poking around some bolts of cloth. The girl was looking awfully pale. He slowed his quick-step, watching more closely as he swerved to approach his destination at an angle that would allow him to watch the kids a little longer. Something about the way that boyfriend looked was a little hinky. Familiar, too.

Yeah. It was the same kid who'd tried to push Ross Malachy around yesterday—the guy with the rust-and-cream-colored van. *Small world,* he thought.

He was almost at the point where he had to change vectors for the tobacconists or find himself in among the shoulder pads and thread and hem tape, when the heavy glass door of the mall slammed open, and Ross Malachy lunged in, scattering exiting shoppers like guinea fowl, squawking.

Lisa didn't want to buy a spool of thread. But Stenno brooked no resistance. His hand on her upper arm was leaving dents. She'd have bruises, she was sure.

So she went with him into the notions shop and dutifully asked the shop owner about matching thread to her mauve T-shirt. Stenno stayed near the shop entrance, peering out into the mall through the window display. The lady was warm and cheerful, not at all annoyed to have a last-minute customer delaying her getting home to her dinner.

"What was it you needed it for, dear?" she said.

She couldn't think of an answer. She didn't want to be here, not really. She knew Stenno wanted her to distract the woman, like he had distracted the department store people so she could take the scarf; but she couldn't imagine what he wanted to steal here.

Distraction. What was the most distracting thing she could think of—

"My mother," she said. The words came first, and then the sharp, precise memory of how her mother looked in the awkward, narrow bed with the side railings. And her father, standing at the end of the bed, looking so sad. So lost. "My mom's got cancer. She's in the hospital."

The woman reacted with instant shock and sympathy and uncertainty. "Oh, dear, that's dreadful." She paused, searching for some kind of response to this unexpected announcement. "Were you planning to make her a present?" she tried helpfully.

A present, yes. Her mother had taught her how to sew ages ago. It was their little conspiracy to keep her out of the home economics classes her father wanted her to attend. Jenniver taught her how to read a pattern and cut material and operate the old Singer sewing machine, and then she would go into the living room to sit. Lisa would go and ask questions when she got stuck. That first quilted bed jacket had come out really well, even if it was two sizes too small. Her mother wanted her to sew more of her clothes, but none of the

247

kids did that kind of thing. They'd laugh at her. Besides, she liked to buy stuff. Pretty stuff. Like that scarf.

But she couldn't give her mother a stolen scarf.

She looked over her shoulder at Stenno, and then away, quickly. This was his idea, not hers.

"I don't know," she whispered.

"Well, did you have a pattern in mind? Maybe something she could use?"

"I don't know what she could use," she said, fingering some decorative rickrack. "I don't know." She couldn't look into the kind, concerned eyes. This was a nice lady, a really nice lady, and Stenno was going to steal from her.

"Okay, get your hands up."

Lisa turned, horrified, to see Stenno standing right behind the shop owner, her father's gun in his hand. His eyes had a crazy glint in them, and the barrel of the gun was buried in the shop owner's carefully styled sleek black hair. Her eyes were huge and terrified, frantically seeking Lisa's as if asking if this could possibly be a joke.

"Stenno!" Lisa yelped. "No!"

And her exclamation was echoed, almost immediately, by the two men elbowing each other aside to get into the shop. One of them was Ross Malachy. The other man, shorter, older, she thought she had never seen before.

But neither one of them had guns, and Stenno did, and he was grinning as if things were happening exactly the way he wanted them to.

"You back off or the old lady gets it!" he said. The shop owner moaned, and he twisted her arm up higher.

He wasn't shouting. The two men skidded to a stop, glanced at each other. The people outside were looking at them curiously, but they couldn't see that much through the display. Just these two guys—they weren't standing quite side by side any more, Lisa noticed; somehow there was more space between them. Stenno had a grin on his face that showed all his teeth, more like a snarl than a smile.

"Lisa, go open up the cash register," he said over his shoulder to her. She could see the store owner shaking. He had one of her arms twisted up behind her. "Go on!"

"Lisa," Ross said. His voice was calm, coaxing. "Lisa, you don't want to do this. You know it's wrong."

"Shut up," Stenno said. He looked over in Lisa's direction. "Go on, open it up."

He watched her as she made her uncertain way around the display stand of laces to the register, so he didn't see the other man, the one Lisa didn't know, take a casual step diagonally away from Ross, away and forward from him. The shop owner's eyes were filled with tears, and she was biting all the lipstick off her lower lip. Stenno was grinning still.

"Lisa," Ross began again. He stopped when Stenno swung back toward him and pointed the gun straight at him.

Sam's mouth was dry with fear as he watched Stenno's hands. The boy's eyes, bright and dilated, gave no clue to whether he'd shoot or not. He had to watch Stenno's hands, watch the muzzle of the gun. He felt that all his senses were hyperacute,

249

that he could hear running footsteps as far away as the other end of the mall, half a mile away. He could smell the food in the garden court, even distinguish between the tomato smells of ketchup and salsa. He could sense the movement of each of the people in the shop before they even began it, Lisa hovering at the cash register as terrified as Mrs. Sanchez was, Stenno coiled and waiting. Al poised, just over an arm's length away.

He felt an almost telepathic communication with Al, as if the link through Ziggy was established not only with the Observer but with Al's earlier self as well. He knew exactly what the other man was attempting to do—split the target, make it more difficult for Stenno to pick one of them to shoot at. And he was good, really good. At least Lisa was out of the line of fire.

"Oh, God, be careful," Al-the-Observer prayed, audible only to Sam and to Whomever the prayer might be directed. "Sam, be careful, please!"

"*You* be careful," Sam muttered, watching the corporate Al sidling another ever-so-cautious few inches away. If the other man could just create enough distance between the two of them, split the target they presented, maybe they could take advantage of Stenno's hesitation in choosing which target to shoot at.

Of course, on the other hand, Stenno might just start shooting, in which case at least one person would die. Almost certainly the store owner; perhaps Lisa.

And maybe Al. Cold sweat broke out on Sam's forehead. If Al died here, who would take the place of the Observer in the future?

If he closed his eyes and concentrated, could he remember that happening before—when the voice reading off the odds changed from the familiar growl to . . . something else? Had Al's own life ever been threatened before in a Leap? He couldn't remember, and he didn't want to risk a glance at his link to his own time. And he *couldn't* risk closing his eyes.

"What are the odds?" he asked, as much to hear the sound of the answer as to hear the answer itself. Stenno would think the question was for him. Al—the Observer—would know better.

Well, one Al would, anyway. He could see the look he was getting from the man inching away to his right. It was okay; he was used to the other man thinking he was nuts. But not at a time like this. He wished there was some way he could explain. Of course, if they all survived, he wouldn't have to. At least, he didn't think so. And if they *didn't* all survive. . . .

"Ninety-two percent that at least one person dies," Al said. The words were clipped, terse. He glared at Stenno.

"And?" Al wasn't telling him everything. He'd known all through this Leap that Al wasn't telling him everything, and he was going to have a heck of a talk with him about that when all this was over.

"And what?" Stenno challenged. "Lisa?"

The lights were beginning to dim in the mall common areas. They could hear the shutdown of stores up and down the hall.

Lisa's gaze was darting back and forth between the gun, the hostage, and Sam. She didn't look at Al, not directly, which told Sam that she had some idea what they were trying to do. He hoped that she would cooperate. The fact that he wasn't sure what form that cooperation should take, and clearly neither did she, was another problem entirely.

"I—I can't get it open," she said. It was an electronic register with a touchpad instead of buttons to push. She was licking her lips and poking ineffectually at the pressure-sensitive squares.

"Ninety-five point four percent," Al said.

"Stenno, somebody might get hurt here," Sam said. He was trying to keep his voice soothing. From the looks of things, if he offered any kind of threat to the boy at all, he would start shooting just for the joy of noise.

Ninety-five point four percent. That *one* person would die. He desperately wanted to know what the odds were that more than one person would die here. And who. For instance, if he was going to die here. Or Al.

He risked a glance at the other man—the physically present other man. Al was poised, balanced, watchful.

"Yeah, somebody's gonna get hurt real bad right here if that cash register doesn't get opened right now!"

With a strangled sob, the store owner fainted, sagging against the boy. Startled, he stepped back, letting the slight body slide to the floor.

Sam smothered a curse. "Where'd you get the gun, Stenno?"

He was stalling like crazy, hoping that mall security would show up and provide some firepower. But no—mall security guards didn't carry guns. If more people came in now, it would only spook the kid worse, increase the chances that somebody would be killed. Abruptly, he reversed tactics, stepping forward boldly.

"Sam!" Al cried out, holding up the handlink. "I don't know what you're trying to do, but it isn't working! The odds have gone up to ninety-seven percent!"

"I can't get it open!" Lisa wailed.

Stenno finally realized that he was being outflanked. He looked wildly from Sam to the Al he could see, and backed away and around the sprawled body over to Lisa, at the cash register. The machine resisted his efforts as well as hers. Cursing, he shoved the girl to one side, raised the gun, and fired.

The explosion reverberated between the walls of the small store, louder in the enclosed space than any of them expected it to be. Lisa shrieked, cowering against the shelves behind the sales desk. Sam lunged, and so did Al. As the smaller man moved he snatched up a fistful of cloth and swung it out like a torero's cape between himself and Sam.

Stenno raised the gun and fired again, and again, and again, the muzzle of the gun wavering between his attackers and the cloth that was somehow a target too, stumbling backward and grabbing for the terrified girl. "Get back or I swear I'll kill her!" he screamed, his voice breaking.

"The hell you will," Al growled. To Sam's ears, it was in stereo. His heart jolted as he saw the gun move, as if in slow motion, the silver muzzle still smoking, still shaking, pointing away from Lisa and directly at Al.

"No!" he yelled, launching himself over the last display. Stenno's line of vision shifted. The muzzle started to follow. Lisa wailed and tried to pull it away.

"Hey!" Al roared. The two of them reached the boy at the same time, struggling to control the weapon. And there was Lisa, in the way, and the muzzle of the gun wavering; somehow it was no surprise to Sam as the gun fired one more time, and Al cried out in anguish.

CHAPTER

TWENTY-FOUR

"Mom!"

Momentarily, Lisa had forgotten her mother's diagnosis. She was a frightened fifteen-year-old who needed comfort, and she threw herself into her mother's arms with abandon. At the end of the bed, her father watched, his hands clenching the end rail, carrying his weight and the weight of the world together.

Sam watched from the doorway, sagging against the frame. Jenniver had her daughter enfolded in her arms, murmuring soothing words into her hair; Stephen was rigid at the end of the bed, swaying forward toward the women and then back, straightening himself, disciplining himself.

"I dunno, Sam," Al murmured in his ear. "You'd think I'd remember getting shot right before retiring like that."

"Are you sure you don't remember?" Sam said

softly, without turning around.

"Well . . ."

Out of the corner of his eye, he could see Al taking off his suit coat, handing it to someone—the coat promptly vanished as Al let go—tucking the handlink under his arm and unbuttoning the cuff of his left sleeve. Gold thread glistened in the Observer's suspenders.

"There's the scar, all right," Al said. "And that bone still aches sometimes. I remember the doctor telling me about that. Change in weather would always get to me, he said."

Sam closed his eyes and smiled to himself, without bitterness. *The more things change, the more they remain the same.*

"What the hell is wrong with that guy?" Al went on, rolling down his sleeve. "Can't he tell he needs to be a part of this? I'll bet that's what you need to do to Leap, Sam. Tell him."

"I don't think so," Sam responded. His fingertips brushed against the bloodstain on his own shirt. There had been a lot of blood. He remembered counting the shots, remembered going for Stenno's throat in blind rage and still thinking there was one more bullet in the gun, but the cylinder was empty. The hammer had snapped down harmlessly, and he had wrestled Stenno to the floor, and mall security had shown up at last, alerted by the gunshots. He'd put a tourniquet on Al's arm, making a real mess of himself in the process, but it didn't matter. He'd managed to talk the cops into letting Lisa go with him to the hospital, following the ambulance. It all seemed so long ago now.

"Ziggy says that Lisa will be okay," Al announced.

"Mrs. Sanchez, the lady in the store, asks for leniency for her. The judge lets her work out her parole in the store—hey, that's pretty neat. And she finishes high school and goes to college."

"What about Stenno?" Sam asked, still watching the Wales family.

Al sighed. "You can't save them all, Sam."

"Got to try," he murmured. "Got to at least *try*."

"Then why don't you get in there?"

"No." He stepped aside to let a night-shift nurse in with a meds cart. Lisa would not be pried away from her mother; every time she tried to get up she collapsed again. She had been a real trouper in the store, once Stenno was down; she'd found a dowel stick to help make the tourniquet and followed Sam's directions to the letter without a tear. She was entitled to break down now.

At least the occupant of the other bed had checked out earlier in the day.

"Are you waiting for something, or what?" Al said, querulous.

"Yeah, you could say that," Sam replied, smiling to himself. He liked logical endings. "And here it comes."

It was Al, dragging an I.V. pole behind him, pale but determined. He'd found his pants. The stained khaki was in perfect style with the hospital gown he wore over it. His arm was splinted and wrapped close against his chest.

"There you are," he said gruffly to Sam. "They said you'd be up here."

"You shouldn't be out of bed," Sam observed, pro forma.

The Admiral snorted. "When they lay me up for a

damned broken arm is the day they'll plant me six feet under. In a Navy hospital I'd already be back in my quarters. They don't mess around in military hospitals."

"No, I don't suppose they do." Sam edged back, giving the injured man a clear view of what was going on in the room.

"Hey, what's going on here?" Al shuffled forward a couple of steps. "Wales?"

Stephen Wales looked up with a mixture of relief and appalled recognition on his face, and releasing the bed rail, came over to shoo the two men—and the hologram, though he didn't know that—out of the doorway, welcoming the excuse to get away.

"It's my wife," he explained in a low voice. "She's very ill."

"Oh, no. I'm really sorry to hear that," Al said. "Is there anything—"

"She doesn't want to have an operation that could save her life," Sam interrupted deliberately. "It's very expensive, and she doesn't feel that it's worthwhile to spend the money."

"Yeah, because *you* aren't in there supporting her," the hologram snapped to the heedless Wales. "Why should she get an operation when the most important thing in *your* life is that stupid encounter group and the family finances?"

"*What?*" Admiral Calavicci, responding to Sam's remark, was sometimes given to hasty judgments. This was one of those times. "That's crazy!"

Dr. Wales looked distinctly uncomfortable.

"I thought so," Sam murmured, watching the other two men. "But Dr. Wales is right, of course. It's her decision. She's the only one who can decide."

258

"Sam, are you nuts? You're acting like you agree with this yutz!" The hologram was outraged. "You have to talk to him!"

Sam shook his head. "It's sad, of course, but every person is ultimately responsible for himself. Right, Dr. Wales?"

"That's right," Wales agreed. "I can't presume to make a decision for Jenniver. It's her life, after all. It's this kind of hard choice that strengthens us, in the long run."

The Admiral was going, as they said in the Navy, ballistic. "Are you telling me that your wife is sitting in there with her little girl and you're just going to stand there and *watch them*?"

The nurses up at the main station were beginning to view the hall conference with unease. One had her hand on a telephone receiver, poised to call someone. Al was so furious his face was getting red, even though he'd suffered considerable blood loss that evening, and he was swaying noticeably, holding himself up with the support of the I.V. rack and an unobtrusive helping hand from Sam.

"A real man doesn't let his emotions get in the way," Wales started. His voice was cracking.

"You can't just stand there! Why are you just standing there?" the hologram sputtered at all of them. "Sam, if she has the operation, Ziggy says there *is* a chance. She's *got* to! And you know as well as I do that she's just waiting for somebody to come and tell her it's worth it!"

Sam shook his head again.

"There's nothing I can do . . . ," Wales whispered. "She has to decide for herself."

"Are you out of your frigging *mind*?" the impatient

patient snarled. "That's your *family* in there!"

"I'm doing what I think is best," Wales offered feebly.

"So help me, I'm gonna do what *I* think is best." The hologram stepped inside his physical self. To Sam's eyes, one image blurred over the other, and he blinked. He blinked again as the hologram-Al grimaced with concentrated effort and took a swing, with his handlink-holding hand, at Wales. He blinked again and stepped back in surprise as the physical hand clenched and rose to follow the hologram's impulse.

"Hey!" The exclamation could have been a chorus from Sam and Stephen Wales.

"Get back in there, you jerk!" Al—Sam couldn't tell which one—was raving.

"*Basta!*" Al raved. "A *real man* doesn't just stand there when his wife and daughter are falling apart! He gets in there and he helps! He offers support! He tells them it's gonna be all right! He takes care of them! He—"

"Okay, okay, okay," Sam interjected. Rack and hand or no, Al was beginning to slide ungracefully to the floor.

"I don't know *how,*" Stephen Wales was saying miserably. He was crying himself now, frozen, unable even to aid Sam in picking up the frothing Al. The nurses were on their way down the hallway, a full phalanx of white-clad avenging angels. "I don't know what to do. I've *told* them I care about them, that it's important that Jenniver get her operation, that—"

"*Gesu e Maria! Bisogna ballare!*" Al squawked, fading fast.

"Huh?" Wales said, understandably confused.

"Oh, he only uses Italian when he's *really* upset," Sam, now down on his knees keeping Al from puddling flat on the floor, assured him. "He's telling you you've got to get back in there and show them you love them. Don't just say it. Show it."

"But how—"

"Go *hug* them," Al snarled, just as the angels descended.

"You know, if you're willing to show your wife how much she means to you, she might be more willing to take the risk of that operation," Sam said thoughtfully.

Wales sniffled, staring after the indignant cluster forcibly moving the patient back to his own room. Then he squared his shoulders, lifted his chin, and marched back into his wife's room.

" 'If you're gonna dance, then *dance,*' " Al, calmer now, translated as he looked after himself being hustled down the hall. He checked his data readout. "The odds are going up, Sam. That Jenniver makes it, I mean."

"I know." Sam was unable to restrain a certain smugness in his voice. The two of them, Leaper and Observer, peeked back into the room.

There was Lisa, standing beside the bed now, her arm still around her mother. And there was Stephen, her father, taking a deep breath and coming up close beside her, putting a tentative hand on her shoulder and patting it, awkwardly.

Both women jumped in surprise, and he flinched back, trying to hide the offending hand behind his back. But it was too late. Lisa had already dragged him into the three-way embrace, and now all three of them were crying, but it was a different kind of tears.

Sam sighed happily.

"Okay, *now* you can Leap?" Al asked.

The two of them looked at each other. And looked. And nothing happened.

"You really think he'd like this?" Lisa said nervously.

"I'm sure."

"Sam, what are you up to?"

It was Monday, June 25, 1990. The morning paper had announced that Iran blamed the U.S. for the earthquake. A Navajo student attending the University of New Mexico had found a "New Gap to Bridge" that was, in fact, as old as the clash of cultures. A New Mexico man had been elected President of the League of United Latin American citizens. It was going to be another hot, dry, sunny day.

"Ross Malachy" and Lisa Wales were on their way up the elevator, bearing gifts. Trailing along behind them, muttering to himself, was Al. He was wearing black slacks, a shirt with large random letters on a black background, and a leopard-print tie. If he had been present in the flesh, as it were, he would be sweltering. Sam had pointed this out to him when he had finally caught up to them, just outside the gift shop. For his part, Al had pointed out that Ziggy liked things really, really cold, and the Imaging Chamber was no picnic. Sam had smiled.

Lisa was trying to juggle flowers and a box. The door opened, and she started to step out, pausing when Sam didn't immediately follow.

"You go ahead," he said. "I'll catch up."

"Oh, are you going to visit me?" Al was visibly pleased. "That's really nice."

262

"I thought so." The elevator let him off at the orthopedic floor, and he made his way quickly down the hall to the proper room.

Admiral Calavicci was nearly as white as the sheets he was lying on, his eyes closed and his left arm dangling from a traction hook to keep it elevated. Shaking his head, Sam sneaked a look at the chart.

"Tsk, tsk."

The brown eyes, dulled a little by medication and pain, opened. "Wha— Oh, it's you."

"Don't try to sit up. I just stopped by to say thank you. You saved my life, you know."

The heavy brows knitted. "Did I? Yeah, I guess I did, didn't I. Well, I was there. You have to use all your available resources, y'know. Next time be a little more careful, okay, kid? I might not be around to save your ass." His eyes closed again.

"Boy, I really looked awful, didn't I?" The Observer was fascinated, examining the details of the suspension arrangement.

"Yes. You took a real chance, rushing him like that for me."

"Guess I need to look before I leap." The Admiral was getting tired.

"Don't we all," Sam murmured, watching as the patient's eyes drifted closed. "You know, that stunt last night really took it out of you," he continued. "You're going to have to take some time to get back on your feet."

The eyes snapped back open, challenged. "What, you think I'm some kind of old man?"

Sam lifted his hands. "No, no, no, nothing like that. It's just that, you know, lots of things are changing

263

for you now, and you've got this broken arm. Makes a great excuse for sitting back a little and taking some time to think about things. You should take advantage of the opportunity."

The eyes narrowed. "What do you know about what's changing for me?"

Sam shrugged. "I dunno. I heard it somewhere. That you were retiring from the military, and . . . that you were retiring. I knew somebody once who was retiring from the military. It wasn't easy, being a civilian all of a sudden."

The Observer was watching Sam now with open admiration. "Oh, you're good, Sam. You're really good."

Sam glanced at him, biting back a grin.

"Well, I can't stay *here*." The patient glanced up at his arm in disgust. "This really sucks."

"You know what I think you should do?" Sam said, the picture of innocence. "Since you really shouldn't stress yourself any more. Right now, I mean," he added hastily. "With a bullet wound. You ought to take some time. That's serious stuff."

"Yeah, kid, what do you think I should do with all this time you think I have?" The words were heavily laced with sarcasm, but not so heavily that it wasn't clear the man in the bed was curious about the answer. He tilted his head, watching as Sam came around the bed to adjust the wires and hooks and trappings so the arm would hang more comfortably.

"I think if you've got any friends in this part of the country, you ought to give them a call. I'll bet they'd be glad to see you. I'll bet they want to see you."

The man in the bed opened his mouth to dismiss

the idea, then closed it again, slowly. "Yeah. I guess I could do that, come to think of it."

"Sure you could. He really wants to hear from you. Like his life depends on it," Sam said cheerfully. "And you wouldn't want to disappoint an old friend, would you?"

"No, I guess not. . . ." The Admiral was still watching him, confused and wary.

"Oh, and I got you a present. Call it a get-well, thank-you-for-saving-my-life, welcome-to-retirement kind of thing."

"Oh yeah?" Suspicion wiped away, Al smiled, and tried again to sit up.

"I'm gonna have to open it for you," Sam warned. He took out a narrow, flat box. "There's a card, see?"

The cover of the card featured a crudely drawn cartoon of a man fairly mummified in bandages. Al opened it with his free hand—"I'm not helpless!"— and both versions read it, in unison. " 'When you leap into the unknown, make sure you've packed your parachute! Get Well Soon!' "

"You didn't sign it," he said. But he was distracted by the box, and set the card aside, watching eagerly as the gray satin ribbon slid off, taking it away from Sam to open it. "What the . . ."

He held up a tie—a fine silk tie, heavy, expensive, beautiful, fluorescent purple with tiny bright pink squares and circles. "Oh, Sam," the Observer breathed. "That's terrific."

"Oh boy," the patient said, awed and appalled in equal measure. "Hey, I'm in the military. I don't wear anything like this."

"You will," Sam assured him. And Leaped.